ACROSS THE

Nightingale Floor

JOURNEY TO INUYAMA

EPISODE
2

FIREBIRD
WHERE FANTASY TAKES FLIGHT™

Across the Nightingale Floor *Episode One: The Sword* *of the Warrior*	Lian Hearn
The Blue Sword	Robin McKinley
The Dreaming Place	Charles de Lint
Firebirds: An Anthology of *Original Fantasy and* *Science Fiction*	Sharyn November, ed.
The Green Man: Tales from *the Mythic Forest*	Ellen Datlow and Terri Windling, eds.
The Hex Witch of Seldom	Nancy Springer
The Mount	Carol Emshwiller
The Riddle of the Wren	Charles de Lint
Spindle's End	Robin McKinley
Tamsin	Peter S. Beagle
Treasure at the Heart *of the Tanglewood*	Meredith Ann Pierce
Waifs and Strays	Charles de Lint
Water: Tales of Elemental Spirits	Robin McKinley and Peter Dickinson

BOOKS BY LIAN HEARN

TALES OF THE OTORI

Across the Nightingale Floor
Episode One: The Sword of the Warrior
Episode Two: Journey to Inuyama

Grass for His Pillow
Episode One: Lord Fujiwara's Treasures
Episode Two: The Way Through the Snow

Brilliance of the Moon
Episode One: Battle for Maruyama
Episode Two: Scars of Victory

OTORI
CLAN

MARUYAMA
CLAN

SEISHUU
CLAN

SHIRAKAWA
CLAN

TOHAN
CLAN

TALES
OF THE

OTORI

EPISODE
2

ACROSS THE
Nightingale Floor
JOURNEY TO INUYAMA

LIAN HEARN

FIREBIRD
AN IMPRINT OF PENGUIN GROUP (USA) INC.

FIREBIRD
Published by the Penguin Group
Penguin Group (USA) Inc., 345 Hudson Street, New York, New York 10014, U.S.A.
Penguin Group (Canada), 10 Alcorn Avenue, Toronto, Ontario, Canada M4V 3B2
(a division of Pearson Penguin Canada Inc.)

Registered Offices: Penguin Books Ltd, 80 Strand, London WC2R 0RL, England

This is a work of fiction. Names, characters, places, and incidents either are the product of the
author's imagination or are used fictitiously, and any resemblance to actual persons, living or dead,
business establishments, events or locales is entirely coincidental.

The author gratefully acknowledges permission to quote from *From the Country of Eight Islands* by
Hiroaki Sato, translated by Burton Watson. Used by permission of Columbia University Press.

First published in the United States of America by Riverhead Books, published by The Berkley
Publishing Group, a division of Penguin Group (USA) Inc., 2002
Published by Firebird, an imprint of Penguin Group (USA) Inc., 2005
Excerpt from *Grass for His Pillow* copyright © Lian Hearn, 2003

1 3 5 7 9 10 8 6 4 2

Copyright © Lian Hearn, 2002
Ornaments drawn by Jackie Aher
Clan symbols by Jackie Aher
Calligraphy drawn by Ms. Sugiyama Kazuko
Map by Xiangyi Mo

All rights reserved

THE LIBRARY OF CONGRESS HAS CATALOGUED THE RIVERHEAD EDITION AS FOLLOWS:
Hearn, Lian.
Across the nightingale floor / Lian Hearn.
p.   cm.—(Tales of the Otori ; bk. 1)
ISBN 1-57322-225-9
1. Teenage boys—Fiction. 2. Orphans—Fiction. 3. Japan—Fiction. I. Title.
PR9619.3.H3725 A65 2002 2002022339
823'.914—dc21

ISBN 0-14-240433-0

Printed in China

To E.

AUTHOR'S NOTE

The books that make up the *Tales of the Otori* are set in an imaginary country in a feudal period. Neither the setting nor the period is intended to correspond to any true historical era, though echoes of many Japanese customs and traditions will be found, and the landscape and seasons are those of Japan. Nightingale floors (*uguisubari*) are real inventions and were constructed around many residences and temples; the most famous examples can be seen in Kyoto at Nijo Castle and Chion'In. I have used Japanese names for places, but these have little connection with real places, apart from Hagi and Matsue, which are more or less in their true geographical positions. As for characters, they are all invented, apart from the artist Sesshu, who seemed impossible to replicate.

I hope I will be forgiven by purists for the liberties I have taken. My only excuse is that this is a work of the imagination.

THE THREE COUNTRIES

N 北

MATSUE

THE EAST

東 Tohan

INUYAMA

Hinode

Mino

——————— *fief boundaries*

·········· *fief boundaries before Yaegahara*

— — — — — *high road*

 battlefields

 castletown

shrine

temple

CHARACTERS

The Clans

THE OTORI
(Middle Country; castle town: Hagi)

Otori Shigeru: rightful heir to the clan

Otori Takeshi: his younger brother, murdered by the Tohan clan **(d.)**

Otori Takeo: (born Tomasu) his adopted son

Otori Shigemori: Shigeru's father, killed at the battle of Yaegahara **(d.)**

Otori Ichiro: a distant relative, Shigeru and Takeo's teacher

Chiyo

Haruka: maids in the household

Shiro: a carpenter

Otori Shoichi: Shigeru's uncle, now lord of the clan

Otori Masahiro: Shoichi's younger brother

Otori Yoshitomi: Masahiro's son

Miyoshi Kahei: brothers, friends of Takeo
Miyoshi Gemba

Miyoshi Satoru: their father, captain of the guard in Hagi castle

Endo Chikara: a senior retainer

Terada Fumifusa: a pirate
Terada Fumio: his son, friend of Takeo

Ryoma: a fisherman, Masahiro's illegitimate son

THE TOHAN
(The East; castle town: Inuyama)

Iida Sadamu: lord of the clan
Iida Nariaki: Sadamu's cousin

Ando, Abe: Iida's retainers

Lord Noguchi: an ally
Lady Noguchi: his wife
Junko: a servant in Noguchi castle

THE SEISHUU
*(An alliance of several ancient families in the West;
main castle towns Kumamoto and Maruyama)*

Arai Daiichi: a warlord

Niwa Satoru: a retainer
Akita Tsutomu: a retainer
Sonoda Mitsuru: Akita's nephew
Maruyama Naomi: head of the Maruyama domain,
    Shigeru's lover

Mariko: her daughter
Sachie: her maid

Sugita Haruki: a retainer
Sugita Hiroshi: his nephew
Sakai Masaki: Hiroshi's cousin

Lord Shirakawa
Kaede: Shirakawa's eldest daughter, Lady Maruyama's cousin
Ai, Hana: Shirakawa's daughters

Ayame
Manami
Akane: maids in the household

Amano Tenzo: a Shirakawa retainer

Shoji Kiyoshi: senior retainer to Lord Shirakawa

The Tribe

THE MUTO FAMILY

Muto Kenji: Takeo's teacher, the Master
Muto Shizuka: Kenji's niece, Arai's mistress, and Kaede's
    companion
Zenko, Taku: her sons
Muto Seiko: Kenji's wife
Muto Yuki: their daughter
Muto Yuzuru: a cousin

Kana
Miyabi: maids

THE KIKUTA FAMILY

Kikuta Isamu: Takeo's real father (d.)
Kikuta Kotaro: his cousin, the Master
Kikuta Gosaburo: Kotaro's younger brother
Kikuta Akio: their nephew
Kikuta Hajime: a wrestler
Sadako: a maid

THE KURODA FAMILY

Kuroda Shintaro: a famous assassin
Kondo Kiichi
Imai Kazuo
Kudo Keiko

Others

Lord Fujiware: a nobleman, exiled from the capital
Mamoru: his protégé and companion
Ono Rieko: his cousin
Murita: a retainer

Matsuda Shingen: the abbot at Terayama
Kubo Makoto: a monk, Takeo's closest friend

Jin-emon: a bandit

Jiro: a farmer's son

Jo-An: an outcast

Horses

Raku: gray with black mane and tail, Takeo's first horse, given by him to Kaede
Kyu: black, Shigeru's horse, disappeared in Inuyama
Aoi: black, half brother to Kyu
Ki: Amano's chestnut
Shun: Takeo's bay, a very clever horse

bold = main characters
(**d.**) = character died before the start of *Across the Nightingale Floor, Episode 1*

天平五年癸酉、遣唐使の船、難波
を発ちて海に入る時に、親母の、子に
贈る歌一首　短歌を并せたり

秋萩を　妻間ふ鹿こそ　独子に

子持てりといへ　鹿児じもの　吾が

独子の　草枕　旅にし行けば

竹珠を　しじに貫き垂り　齋瓮に

木綿取り垂でて　齋ひつつ

思ふ吾子　真幸くありこそ

「万葉集」巻九
一七九〇
一七九一

The deer that weds

The autumn bush clover

They say

Sires a single fawn

And this fawn of mine

This lone boy

Sets off on a journey

Grass for his pillow

MANYOSHU VOL. 9,
NO. 1,790

ACROSS THE

Nightingale Floor

JOURNEY TO INUYAMA

· 1 ·

After my formal adoption into the clan, I began to see more of the young men of my own age from warrior families. Ichiro was much sought after as a teacher, and since he was already instructing me in history, religion, and the classics, he agreed to take on other pupils as well. Among these was Miyoshi Gemba, who, with his older brother, Kahei, was to become one of my closest allies and friends. Gemba was a year older than me. Kahei was already in his twenties, and too old for Ichiro's instruction, but he helped teach the younger men the arts of war.

For these I now joined the men of the clan in the great hall opposite the castle, where we fought with poles and studied other martial arts. On its sheltered southern side was a wide field for horsemanship and archery. I was no better with the bow than I'd ever been, but I could acquit myself well enough with the pole and the sword. Every morning, after two hours of writing practice with Ichiro, I would ride with a couple of men through the winding streets of the castle town and spend four or five hours in relentless training.

In the late afternoons I returned to Ichiro with his other pupils, and we struggled to keep our eyes open while he tried to teach us the principles of Kung Tzu and the history of the Eight Islands. The summer solstice passed, and the Festival of the Weaver Star, and the days of the great heat began. The plum rains had ended, but it remained very humid, and heavy storms threatened. The farmers gloomily predicted a worse than usual typhoon season.

My lessons with Kenji also continued, but at night. He stayed away from the clan hall, and warned me against revealing my Tribe skills.

"The warriors think it's sorcery," he said. "They'll despise you for it."

We went out on many nights, and I learned to move invisibly through the sleeping town. We had a strange relationship. I did not trust him at all in daylight. I'd been adopted by the Otori, and I'd given my heart to them. I did not want to be reminded that I was an outsider, even a freak. But it was different at night. Kenji's skills were unparalleled. He wanted to share them with me, and I was mad with hunger to learn them—partly for their own sake, because they fulfilled some dark need that was born into me, and partly because I knew how much I had to learn if I was ever to achieve what Lord Shigeru wanted me to do. Although he had not yet spoken of it to me, I could think of no other reason why he had rescued me from Mino. I was the son of an assassin, a member of the Tribe, now his adopted son. I was going with him to Inuyama. What other purpose could there be but to kill Iida?

Most of the boys accepted me, for Shigeru's sake, and I realized what a high regard they and their fathers had for him. But the sons of Masahiro and Shoichi gave me a hard time, especially Masahiro's oldest son, Yoshitomi. I grew to hate them as much as I hated their fathers, and I despised them, too, for their arrogance and blindness. We often fought with the poles. I knew their intentions towards me were murderous. Once Yoshitomi would have killed me if I had not in an instant used my second self to distract him. He never forgave me for it and often whispered insults to me: Sorcerer. Cheat. I was actually less afraid of him killing me than of having to kill him in self-defense or by accident. No doubt it improved my swordsmanship, but I was relieved when the time for our departure came and no blood had been shed.

It was not a good time for traveling, being in the hottest days of summer, but we had to be in Inuyama before the Festival of the Dead began. We did not take the direct highway through Yamagata, but went south to Tsuwano, now the outpost town of the Otori fief, on the road to the West, where we would meet the bridal party and where the betrothal would take place. From there we would cross into Tohan territory and pick up the post road at Yamagata.

Our journey to Tsuwano was uneventful and enjoyable despite the heat. I was away from Ichiro's teaching and from the pressures of training. It was like a holiday, riding in Shigeru and Kenji's company, and for a few days we all seemed to put aside our misgivings of what lay ahead. The rain held off, though lightning flickered round the ranges all night, turning the clouds indigo, and the full summer foliage of the forests surrounded us in a sea of green.

We rode into Tsuwano at midday, having risen at sunrise for the last leg of the journey. I was sorry to arrive, knowing it meant the end of the innocent pleasures of our lighthearted travel. I could not have imagined what was going to take their place. Tsuwano sang of water, its streets lined with canals teeming with fat golden and red carp. We were not far from the inn when suddenly, above the water and the sounds of the bustling town, I clearly heard my own name spoken by a woman. The voice came from a long, low building with white walls and lattice windows, some kind of fighting hall. I knew there were two women inside but I could not see them, and I wondered briefly why they were there, and why one of them should have said my name.

When we came to the inn I heard the same woman talking in the courtyard. I realized she was Lady Shirakawa's maid, and we learned the lady was unwell. Kenji went to her and came back wanting to describe her beauty at length, but the storm broke, and I was afraid the thunder would make the horses restive, so I hurried off to the stables without listening to him. I did not want to hear of her beauty. If I thought about her at all, it was with dislike, for the part she was to play in the trap set for Shigeru.

After a while Kenji caught up with me in the stables, and brought the maid with him. She looked like a pretty, good-natured, scatterbrained girl, but even before she grinned at me in a less than respectful way and addressed me as "Cousin!" I'd picked her as a member of the Tribe.

She held her hands up against mine. "I am also Kikuta, on my mother's side. But Muto on my father's. Kenji is my uncle."

Our hands had the same long-fingered shape and the same line straight across the palm. "That's the only trait I inherited," she said ruefully. "The rest of me is pure Muto."

Like Kenji, she had the power to change her appearance so that you were never sure you recognized her. At first I thought she was very young; in fact she was almost thirty and had two sons.

"Lady Kaede is a little better," she told Kenji. "Your tea made her sleep, and now she insists on getting up."

"You worked her too hard," Kenji said, grinning. "What were you thinking of, in this heat?" To me he added, "Shizuka is teaching Lady Shirakawa the sword. She can teach you too. We'll be here for days in this rain."

He turned back to her. "Maybe you can teach him ruthlessness," he said. "It's all he lacks."

"It's hard to teach," Shizuka replied. "You either have it, or not."

"She has it," Kenji told me. "Stay on her right side!"

I didn't reply. I was a little irritated that Kenji should point out my weakness to Shizuka as soon as we met her. We stood under the eaves of the stable yard, the rain drumming on the cobbles before us, the horses stamping behind.

"Are these fevers a common thing?" Kenji asked.

"Not really. This is the first of its kind. But she is not strong. She hardly eats; she sleeps badly. She frets over the marriage and over her family. Her mother is dying, and she has not seen her since she was seven."

"You have become fond of her," Kenji said, smiling.

"Yes, I have, although I only came to her because Arai asked me to."

"I've never seen a more beautiful girl," Kenji admitted.

"Uncle! You are really smitten by her!"

"I must be getting old," he said. "I find myself moved by her plight. However things work out, she will be the loser."

A huge clap of thunder broke over our heads. The horses bucked and plunged on their lines. I ran to quiet them. Shizuka returned to the inn and Kenji went in search of the

7

bathhouse. I did not see them again until evening.

Later, bathed and dressed in formal robes, I attended on Lord Shigeru for the first meeting with his future wife. We had brought gifts, and I unpacked them from the boxes, together with the lacquerware that we carried with us. A betrothal should be a happy occasion, I suppose, although I had never been to one before. Maybe for the bride it is always a time of apprehension. This one seemed to me to be fraught with tension and full of bad omens.

Lady Maruyama greeted us as if we were no more than slight acquaintances, but her eyes hardly left Shigeru's face. I thought she had aged since I'd met her in Chigawa. She was no less beautiful, but suffering had etched her face with its fine lines. Both she and Shigeru seemed cold, to each other and to everyone else, especially to Lady Shirakawa.

Her beauty silenced us. Despite Kenji's enthusiasm earlier, I was quite unprepared for it. I thought then that I understood Lady Maruyama's suffering: At least part of it had to be jealousy. How could any man refuse the possession of such beauty? No one could blame Shigeru if he accepted it: He would be fulfilling his duty to his uncles and the demands of the alliance. But the marriage would deprive

Lady Maruyama of not only the man she had loved for years but also her strongest ally.

The undercurrents in the room made me uncomfortable and awkward. I saw the pain Lady Maruyama's coldness caused Kaede, saw the flush rise in her cheeks, making her skin lovelier than ever. I could hear her heartbeat and her rapid breath. She did not look at any of us, but kept her eyes cast down. I thought, *She is so young, and terrified.* Then she raised her eyes and looked at me for a moment. I felt she was like a person drowning in the river, and if I reached out my hand I would save her.

"So, Shigeru, you have to choose between the most powerful woman in the Three Countries and the most beautiful," Kenji said later while we were sitting up talking, and after many flasks of wine had been shared. Since the rain seemed likely to keep us in Tsuwano for some days, there was no need to go to bed early in order to rise before dawn. "I should have been born a lord."

"You have a wife, if only you stayed with her," Shigeru replied.

"My wife is a good cook, but she has a wicked tongue, she's fat, and she hates traveling," Kenji grumbled. I said nothing, but laughed to myself, already knowing how Kenji profited from his wife's absence: in the pleasure quarter.

Kenji continued to joke, with, I thought, some deeper purpose of sounding Shigeru out, but the lord replied to him in the same vein, as if he truly were celebrating his betrothal. I went to sleep, fuddled by the wine, to the sound of rain pelting on the roof, cascading down the gutters and over the cobbles. The canals ran to the brim; in the distance I could hear the song of the river grow to a shout as it tumbled down the mountain.

I woke in the middle of the night and was immediately aware that Shigeru was no longer in the room. When I listened I could hear his voice, talking to Lady Maruyama, so low that no one could hear it but me. I had heard them speak like that nearly a year before, in another inn room. I was both appalled at the risk they were taking and amazed at the strength of the love that sustained them through such infrequent meetings.

He will never marry Shirakawa Kaede, I thought, but did not know if this realization delighted me or alarmed me.

I was filled with unease and lay awake till dawn. It was a gray, wet dawn, too, with no sign of any break in the weather. A typhoon, earlier than usual, had swept across the western part of the country, bringing downpours, floods, broken bridges, impassable roads. Everything was damp and smelled of mold. Two of the horses had hot, swollen hocks, and a groom had been kicked in the chest. I ordered poultices for the horses and arranged for an apothecary to see the man. I was eating a late breakfast when Kenji came to remind me about sword practice. It was the last thing I felt like doing.

"What else do you plan to do all day," he demanded, "sit around and drink tea? Shizuka can teach you a lot. We might as well make the most of being stuck here."

So I obediently finished eating and followed my teacher, running through the rain to the fighting school. I could hear the thump and clash of the sticks from outside. Inside, two young men were fighting. After a moment I realized one was not a boy but Shizuka: She was more skillful than her opponent, but the other, taller and with greater determination, was making it quite a good match. At our appearance, though, Shizuka easily got beneath the guard. It wasn't until the other took off the mask that I realized it was Kaede.

"Oh," she said angrily, wiping her face on her sleeve, "they distracted me."

"Nothing must distract you, lady," Shizuka said. "It's your main weakness. You lack concentration. There must be nothing but you, your foe, and the swords."

She turned to greet us. "Good morning, Uncle! Good morning, Cousin!"

We returned the greeting and bowed more respectfully to Kaede. Then there was a short silence. I was feeling awkward: I had never seen women in a fighting hall before—never seen them dressed in practice clothes. Their presence unnerved me. I thought there was probably something unseemly about it. I should not be here with Shigeru's betrothed wife.

"We should come back another time," I said, "when you have finished."

"No, I want you to fight with Shizuka," Kenji said. "Lady Shirakawa can hardly return to the inn alone. It will profit her to watch."

"It would be good for the lady to practice against a man," Shizuka said, "since if it comes to battle, she will not be able to choose her opponents."

I glanced at Kaede and saw her eyes widen slightly, but she said nothing.

"Well, she should be able to beat Takeo," Kenji said sourly. I thought he must have a headache from the wine, and indeed, I myself felt a little the worse for wear.

Kaede sat on the floor, cross-legged like a man. She untied the ties that held back her hair and it fell around her, reaching the ground. I tried not to look at her.

Shizuka gave me a pole and took up her first stance.

We sparred a bit, neither of us giving anything away. I'd never fought with a woman before, and I was reluctant to go all out in case I hurt her. Then, to my surprise, when I feinted one way she was already there, and a twisting upwards blow sent the pole out of my hands. If I'd been fighting Masahiro's son, I'd have been dead.

"Cousin," she said reprovingly. "Don't insult me, please."

I tried harder after that, but she was skillful and amazingly strong. It was only after the second bout that I began to get the upper hand, and then only after her instruction. She conceded the fourth bout, saying, "I have already fought all morning with Lady Kaede. You are fresh, Cousin, as well as being half my age."

13

"A little more than half, I think!" I panted. Sweat was pouring off me. I took a towel from Kenji and wiped myself down.

Kaede said, "Why do you call Lord Takeo 'Cousin'?"

"Believe it or not, we are related, on my mother's side," Shizuka said. "Lord Takeo was not born an Otori, but adopted."

Kaede looked seriously at the three of us. "There is a likeness between you. It's hard to place exactly. But there is something mysterious, as though none of you is what you seem to be."

"The world being what it is, that is wisdom, lady," Kenji said, rather piously, I thought. I imagined he did not want Kaede to know the true nature of our relationship: that we were all from the Tribe. I did not want her to know either. I much preferred her to think of me as one of the Otori.

Shizuka took up the cords and tied back Kaede's hair. "Now you should try against Takeo."

"No," I said immediately. "I should go now. I have to see to the horses. I must see if Lord Otori needs me."

Kaede stood. I was aware of her trembling slightly, and acutely aware of her scent, a flowery fragrance with her sweat beneath it.

"Just one bout," Kenji said. "It can't do any harm."

Shizuka went to put on Kaede's mask, but she waved her away.

"If I am to fight men, I must fight without a mask," she said.

I took up the pole reluctantly. The rain was pouring down even more heavily. The room was dim, the light greenish. We seemed to be in a world within a world, isolated from the real one, bewitched.

It started like an ordinary practice bout, both of us trying to unsettle the other, but I was afraid of hitting her face, and her eyes never left mine. We were both tentative, embarking on something utterly strange to us whose rules we did not know. Then, at some point I was hardly aware of, the fight turned into a kind of dance. Step, strike, parry, step. Kaede's breath came more strongly, echoed by mine, until we were breathing in unison, and her eyes became brighter and her face more glowing, each blow became stronger, and the rhythm of our steps fiercer. For a while I would dominate, then she, but neither of us could get the upper hand. Did either of us want to?

Finally, almost by mistake, I got around her guard and,

15

to avoid hitting her face, let the pole fall to the ground. Immediately, Kaede lowered her own pole and said, "I concede."

"You did well," Shizuka said, "but I think Takeo could have tried a little harder."

I stood and stared at Kaede, open-mouthed like an idiot. I thought, *If I don't hold her in my arms now, I will die.*

Kenji handed me a towel and gave me a rough push in the chest. "Takeo . . ." he started to say.

"What?" I said stupidly.

"Just don't complicate things!"

Shizuka said, as sharply as if she were warning of danger, "Lady Kaede!"

"What?" Kaede said, her eyes still fixed on my face.

"I think we've done enough for one day," Shizuka said. "Let's return to your room."

Kaede smiled at me, suddenly unguarded. "Lord Takeo," she said.

"Lady Shirakawa." I bowed to her, trying to be formal, but utterly unable to keep myself from smiling back at her.

"Well, that's torn it," Kenji muttered.

"What do you expect, it's their age!" Shizuka replied. "They'll get over it."

As Shizuka led Kaede from the hall, calling to the servants who were waiting outside to bring umbrellas, it dawned on me what they were talking about. They were right in one thing, and wrong in another. Kaede and I had been scorched by desire for each other, more than desire, love, but we would never get over it.

For a week the torrents of rain kept us penned up in the mountain town. Kaede and I did not train together again. I wished we had never done so: It had been a moment of madness, I had never wanted it, and now I was tormented by the results. I listened for her all day long, I could hear her voice, her step, and at night—when only a thin wall separated us—her breathing. I could tell how she slept (restlessly) and when she woke (often). We spent time together—we were forced to by the smallness of the inn, by being in the same traveling party, by being expected to be with Lord Shigeru and Lady Maruyama—but we had no opportunity to speak to each other. We were both, I think, equally terrified of giving our feelings away. We hardly dared look at each other, but occasionally our eyes would meet, and the fire leaped between us again.

I went lean and hollow-eyed with desire, made worse by lack of sleep, for I reverted to my old Hagi ways and went exploring at night. Shigeru did not know, for I left while he was with Lady Maruyama, and Kenji either did not or pretended not to notice. I felt I was becoming as insubstantial as a ghost. By day I studied and drew; by night I went in search of other people's lives, moving through the small town like a shadow. Often the thought came to me that I would never have a life of my own, but would always belong to the Otori or to the Tribe.

I watched merchants calculating the loss the water damage would bring them. I watched the townspeople drink and gamble in bars and let prostitutes lead them away by the arm. I watched parents sleep, their children between them. I climbed walls and drainpipes, walked over roofs and along fences. Once I swam the moat, climbed the castle walls and gate, and watched the guards, so close I could smell them. It amazed me that they did not see or hear me. I listened to people talking, awake and in their sleep, heard their protestations, their curses, and their prayers.

I went back to the inn before dawn, drenched to the skin, took off my wet clothes, and slipped naked and shivering beneath the quilts. I dozed and listened to the place waking around me. First the cocks crowed, then the crows began cawing; servants woke and fetched water; clogs clattered over the wooden bridges; Raku and the other horses whinnied from the stables. I waited for the moment when I would hear Kaede's voice.

The rain poured down for three days and then began to lessen. Many people came to the inn to speak to Shigeru. I listened to the careful conversations and tried to discern who was loyal to him and who would be only too eager to join in his betrayal. We went to the castle to present gifts to Lord Kitano, and I saw in daylight the walls and gate I had climbed at night.

He greeted us with courtesy and expressed his sympathy for Takeshi's death. It seemed to be on his conscience, for he returned to the subject more than once. He was of an age with the Otori lords and had sons the same age as Shigeru. They did not attend the meeting. One was said to be away, the other unwell. Apologies were expressed, which I knew were lies.

"They lived in Hagi when they were boys," Shigeru told me later. "We trained and studied together. They came many times to my parents' house and were as close as brothers to Takeshi and myself." He was silent for a moment, then went on: "Well, that was many years ago. Times change and we must all change with them."

But I could not be so resigned. I felt bitterly that the closer we came to Tohan territory, the more isolated he was becoming.

It was early evening. We had bathed and were waiting for the meal. Kenji had gone to the public bathhouse, where a girl had taken his fancy, he said. The room gave on to a small garden. The rain had lessened to a drizzle and the doors were wide open. There was a strong smell of sodden earth and wet leaves.

"It will clear tomorrow," Shigeru said. "We will be able to ride on, but we will not get to Inuyama before the festival. We will be forced to stay in Yamagata, I think." He smiled entirely mirthlessly and said, "I shall be able to commemorate my brother's death in the place where he died. But I cannot let anyone know my feelings. I must pretend to have put aside all thought of revenge."

"Why go into Tohan territory?" I asked. "It's not too late to turn back. If it's my adoption that binds you to the marriage, I could go away with Kenji. It's what he wants."

"Certainly not!" he replied. "I've given my word to these arrangements and set my seal on them. I have plunged into the river now and must go where the current takes me. I would sooner Iida killed me than despised me." He looked around the room, listening. "Are we completely alone? Can you hear anyone?"

I could hear the usual evening sounds of the inn: the soft tread of maids as they carried food and water; from the kitchen, the sound of the cook's knife chopping; water boiling; the muttered conversation of the guards in the passageway and the courtyard. I could hear no other breath but our own.

"We are alone."

"Come closer. Once we are among the Tohan, we will have no chance to talk. There are many things I need to tell you before . . ." He grinned at me, a real smile this time. ". . . before whatever happens in Inuyama!

"I've thought about sending you away. Kenji desires it for your safety, and of course his fears are justified. I must go to

Inuyama, come what may. However, I am asking an almost impossible service from you, far beyond any obligation you may have to me, and I feel I must give you a choice. Before we ride into Tohan territory, after you have heard what I have to say, if you wish to leave with Kenji and join the Tribe, you are free to do so."

I was saved from answering by a faint sound from the passageway. "Someone is coming to the door." We were both silent.

A few moments later the maids entered with trays of food. When they had left again, we began to eat. The food was sparse, because of the rain—some sort of soused fish, rice, devil's tongue, and pickled cucumbers—but I don't think either of us tasted it.

"You may wonder what my hatred of Iida is based on," Shigeru said. "I have always had a personal dislike for him, for his cruelty and double-dealing. After Yaegahara and my father's death, when my uncles took over the leadership of the clan, many people thought I should have taken my own life. That would have been the honorable thing to do—and, for them, a convenient solution to my irritating presence. But as the Tohan moved into what had been Otori land, and I saw the devastating effect of their rule on the common people, I decided a more worthwhile response would be to live and seek revenge. I believe the test of government is the contentment of the people. If the ruler is just, the land receives the blessings of Heaven. In Tohan lands the people are starving, debt-ridden, harassed all the time by Iida's officials. The Hidden are tortured and murdered—crucified, suspended upside down over pits of waste, hung in baskets for the crows to feed on. Farmers have to expose their newborn children and sell their daughters because they have nothing to feed them with."

He took a piece of fish and ate it fastidiously, his face impassive.

"Iida became the most powerful ruler in the Three Countries. Power brings its own legitimacy. Most people believe any lord has the right to do as he pleases in his own clan and his own country. It's what I, too, was brought up to believe in. But he threatened my land, my father's land, and I was not going see it handed over to him without a fight.

"This had been in my mind for many years. I took on a personality for myself that is only partly my own. They call me Shigeru the Farmer. I devoted myself to improving my

land and talked of nothing but the seasons, crops, and irri-
gation. These matters interest me anyway, but they also gave
me the excuse to travel widely through the fief and learn
many things I would not otherwise have known.

"I avoided Tohan lands, apart from yearly visits to
Terayama, where my father and many of my ancestors are
buried. The temple was ceded to the Tohan, along with the
city of Yamagata after Yaegahara. But then the Tohan cruelty
touched me personally, and my patience began to wear thin.

"Last year, just after the Festival of the Weaver Star, my
mother fell ill with a fever. It was particularly virulent: She
was dead within a week. Three other members of the household died, including her maid. I also became sick. For four
weeks I hovered between life and death, delirious, knowing
nothing. I was not expected to recover, and when I did, I
wished I had died, for it was then that I learned my brother
had been killed in the first week of my illness.

"It was high summer. He was already buried. No one
could tell me what had happened. There seemed to be no
witnesses. He had recently taken a new lover, but the girl had
disappeared too. We heard only that a Tsuwano merchant
had recognized his body in the streets of Yamagata and had

arranged burial at Terayama. In desperation I wrote to Muto Kenji, whom I had known since Yaegahara, thinking the Tribe might have some information. Two weeks later a man came to my house late at night, bearing a letter of introduction with Kenji's seal. I would have taken him for a groom or a foot soldier; he confided in me that his name was Kuroda, which I knew can be a Tribe name.

"The girl Takeshi had fallen for was a singer, and they had gone together to Tsuwano for the Star Festival. That much I knew already, for as soon as my mother fell sick, I'd sent word to him not to return to Hagi. I'd meant for him to stay in Tsuwano, but it seems the girl wished to go on to Yamagata, where she had relatives, and Takeshi went with her. Kuroda told me that there were comments made in an inn— insults to the Otori, to myself. A fight broke out. Takeshi was an excellent swordsman. He killed two men and wounded several others, who ran away. He went back to the girl's relatives' house. Tohan men returned in the middle of the night and set fire to the house. Everyone in it burned to death or was stabbed as they tried to escape the flames."

I closed my eyes briefly, thinking I could hear their screams.

"Yes, it was like Mino," Shigeru said bitterly. "The Tohan claimed the family were Hidden, though it seems almost certain they were not. My brother was in traveling clothes. No one knew his identity. His body lay in the street for two days."

He sighed deeply. "There should have been outrage. Clans have gone to war over less. At the very least, Iida should have apologized, punished his men, and made some restitution. But Kuroda reported to me that when Iida heard the news, his words were 'One less of those Otori upstarts to worry about. Too bad it wasn't the brother.' Even the men who committed the act were astonished, Kuroda said. They had not known who Takeshi was. When they found out, they expected their lives to be forfeit.

"But Iida did nothing, nor did my uncles. I told them in private what Kuroda had told me. They chose not to believe me. They reminded me of the rashness of Takeshi's behavior in the past, the fights he had been involved in, the risks he took. They forbade me from speaking publicly about the matter, reminding me that I was still far from well and suggesting I should go away for a while, make a trip to the eastern mountains, try the hot springs, pray at the shrines.

"I decided I would go away, but not for the purposes they suggested."

"You came to find me in Mino," I whispered.

He did not answer me at once. It was dark outside now, but there was a faint glow from the sky. The clouds were breaking up, and between them the moon appeared and disappeared. For the first time I could make out the outline of the mountains and the pine trees, black against the night sky.

"Tell the servants to bring lights," Shigeru said, and I went to the door to call the maids. They came and removed the trays, brought tea, and lit the lamps in the stands. When they had left once more, we drank the tea in silence. The bowls were a dark blue glaze. Shigeru turned his in his hand and then upended it to read the potter's name. "It's not as pleasing to my mind as the earth colors of Hagi," he said, "but beautiful nonetheless."

"May I ask you a question?" I said, and then fell silent again, not sure if I wanted to know the answer.

"Go on," he prompted.

"You have allowed people to believe we met by accident, but I felt you knew where to find me. You were looking for me."

He nodded. "Yes, I knew who you were as soon as I saw

you on the path. I had come to Mino with the express purpose of finding you."

"Because my father was an assassin?"

"That was the main reason, but not the only one."

I felt as if there were not enough air in the room for me to draw the breath I needed. I did not bother with whatever other reasons Lord Shigeru might have had. I needed to concentrate on the main one.

"But how did you know, when I myself did not know— when the Tribe did not know?"

He said, his voice lower than ever, "Since Yaegahara, I have had time to learn many things. I was just a boy then, a typical warrior's son, with no ideas beyond the sword and my family's honor. I met Muto Kenji there, and in the months afterwards he opened my eyes to the power that lay beneath the warrior class's rule. I discovered something about the networks of the Tribe, and I saw how they controlled the warlords and the clans. Kenji became a friend, and through him I met many other Tribe members. They interested me. I probably know more about them than any other outsider. But I've kept this knowledge to myself, never telling anyone else. Ichiro knows a little, and now you do too."

I thought of the heron's beak plunging down into the water.

"Kenji was wrong, the first night he came to Hagi. I knew very well who I was bringing into my household. I had not realized, though, that your talents would be so great." He smiled at me, the openhearted smile that transformed his face. "That was an unexpected reward."

Now I seemed to have lost the power of speech again. I knew we had to broach the subject of Shigeru's purpose in seeking me out and saving my life, but I could not bring myself to speak so baldly of such things. I felt the darkness of my Tribe nature rise within me. I said nothing and waited.

Shigeru said, "I knew I would have no rest under Heaven while my brother's murderers lived. I held their lord responsible for their actions. And in the meantime, circumstances had changed. Arai's falling-out with Noguchi meant the Seishuu were again interested in an alliance with the Otori against Iida. Everything seemed to point to one conclusion: that the time had come to assassinate him."

Once I heard the words, a slow excitement began to burn within me. I remembered the moment in my village when I decided I was not going to die but live and seek revenge—the night in Hagi, under the winter moon, when I had known I had the ability and the will to kill Iida. I felt the stirrings of deep pride that Lord Shigeru had sought me out for this purpose. All the threads of my life seemed to lead towards it.

"My life is yours," I said. "I will do whatever you want."

"I'm asking you to do something extremely dangerous, almost impossible. If you choose not to do it, you may leave with Kenji tomorrow. All debts between us are canceled. No one will think the less of you."

"Please don't insult me," I said, and made him laugh.

I heard steps in the yard and a voice on the veranda. "Kenji is back."

A few moments later he came into the room, followed by a maid bringing fresh tea. He looked us over while she poured it and, once she had left, said, "You look like conspirators. What have you been plotting?"

"Our visit to Inuyama," Shigeru replied. "I have told Takeo my intentions. He is coming with me of his own free will."

Kenji's expression changed. "To his death," he muttered.

"Maybe not," I said lightly. "I am not boasting, but if anyone can get near Lord Iida, it will be me."

"You're just a boy," my teacher snorted. "I've told Lord Shigeru this already. He knows all my objections to this rash plan. Now I'll tell you. Do you really think you'll be able to kill Iida? He's survived more assassination attempts than I've had girls. You are yet to kill anyone! Added to which, there's every chance that you'll be recognized either in the capital or along the way. I believe your peddler did talk about you to someone. It was no accident that Ando turned up in Hagi. He came to check out the rumor and saw you with Shigeru. It's my guess Iida already knows who and where you are. You're likely to be arrested as soon as you enter Tohan territory."

"Not if he is with me, one of the Otori coming to make a friendly alliance," the lord said. "Anyway, I've told him that he's free to go away with you. It's by his own choice that he comes with me."

I thought I detected a note of pride in his voice. I said to Kenji, "There is no question of me leaving. I must go to Inuyama. And anyway, I have scores of my own to settle."

He sighed sharply. "Then I suppose I'll have to go with you."

"The weather has cleared. We can move on tomorrow," Shigeru said.

"There's one other thing I must tell you, Shigeru. You astonished me by keeping your affair with Lady Maruyama hidden for so long. I heard something in the bathhouse, a joke, that makes me believe it is no longer a secret."

"What did you hear?"

"One man, having his back scrubbed, remarked to the girl that Lord Otori was in town with his future wife, and she replied, 'His current wife as well.' Many laughed as if they got her meaning, and went on to speak of Lady Maruyama, and Iida's desire for her. Of course, we are still in Otori country; they have nothing but admiration for you, and they like this rumor. It enhances the Otori reputation and is like a knife in the ribs for the Tohan. All the more reason for it to be repeated until it reaches Iida's ears."

I could see Shigeru's face in the lamplight. There was a curious expression on it. I thought I could read pride there as well as regret.

"Iida may kill me," he said, "but he cannot change the fact that she prefers me over him."

"You are in love with death, like all your class," Kenji said, a depth of anger in his voice that I had never heard before.

"I have no fear of death," Shigeru replied. "But it is

wrong to say I am in love with it. Quite the opposite: I think I've proved how much I love life. But it is better to die than to live with shame, and that is the point I have come to now."

I could hear footsteps approaching. I turned my head like a dog, and both men fell silent. There was a tap on the door and it slid open. Sachie knelt in the entrance. Shigeru immediately rose and went to her. She whispered something and went quietly away. He turned to us and said, "Lady Maruyama wishes to discuss tomorrow's travel arrangements. I will go to her room for a while."

Kenji said nothing, but bowed his head slightly.

"It may be our last time together," Shigeru said softly, and stepped into the passage, sliding the door closed behind him.

"I should have got to you first, Takeo," Kenji grumbled. "Then you would never have become a lord, never been tied to Shigeru by bonds of loyalty. You would be Tribe through and through. You wouldn't think twice about taking off with me now, tonight."

"If Lord Otori had not got to me first, I would be dead!" I replied fiercely. "Where was the Tribe when the Tohan were murdering my people and burning my home? He saved my life then. That's why I cannot leave him. I never will. Never ask me again!"

Kenji's eyes went opaque. "Lord Takeo," he said ironically.

The maids came to spread the beds, and we did not speak again.

The following morning the roads out of Tsuwano were crowded. Many travelers were taking advantage of the finer weather to resume their journey. The sky was a clear deep blue and the sun drew moisture from the earth until it steamed. The stone bridge across the river was undamaged, but the water ran wild and high, throwing tree branches, planks of wood, dead animals and other corpses, possibly, against the piers. I was thinking fleetingly of the first time I'd crossed the bridge at Hagi when I saw a drowned heron floating in the water, its gray and white feathers waterlogged, all its gracefulness crumpled and broken. The sight of it chilled me. I thought it a terrible omen.

The horses were rested and stepped out eagerly. If Shigeru was less eager, if he shared my forebodings, he gave no sign of it. His face was calm, his eyes bright. He seemed to glow with energy and life. It made my heart twist to look at him—made me feel his life and his future all lay in my assassin hands. I looked at my hands as they lay against Raku's pale gray neck and black mane and wondered if they would let me down.

I saw Kaede only briefly, as she stepped into the palanquin outside the inn. She did not look at me. Lady Maruyama acknowledged our presence with a slight bow but did not speak. Her face was pale, her eyes dark-ringed, but she was composed and calm.

It was a slow, laborious journey. Tsuwano had been protected from the worst of the storm behind its mountain barriers, but as we descended into the valley the full extent of the damage became clear. Houses and bridges had been washed away, trees uprooted, fields flooded. The village people watched us, sullen or with open anger, as we rode through the midst of their suffering, and added to it by commandeering their hay to feed our horses, their boats to carry us across the swollen rivers. We were already days overdue and had to press on at whatever cost.

It took us three days to reach the fief border, twice as long as expected. An escort had been sent to meet us here:

one of Iida's chief retainers, Abe, with a group of thirty Tohan men, outnumbering the twenty Otori Lord Shigeru rode with. Sugita and the other Maruyama men had returned to their own domain after our meeting in Tsuwano.

Abe and his men had been waiting a week and were impatient and irritable. They did not want to spend the time that the Festival of the Dead required in Yamagata. There was little love lost between the two clans; the atmosphere became tense and strained. The Tohan men were arrogant and swaggering. We Otori were made to feel that we were inferior, coming as supplicants, not equals. My blood boiled on Shigeru's behalf, but he seemed unmoved, remaining as courteous as usual, and only slightly less cheerful.

I was as silent as in the days when I could not speak. I listened for snatches of conversation that would reveal, like straws, the direction of the wind. But in Tohan country, people were taciturn and close. They knew spies were everywhere and walls had ears. Even when the Tohan men got drunk at night, they did so silently, unlike the noisy, cheerful fashion of the Otori.

I had not been so close to the triple oak leaf since the day of the massacre at Mino. I kept my eyes down and my face averted, afraid I would see or be recognized by one of the men who had burned my village and murdered my family. I used my disguise as an artist, frequently taking out my brushes and ink stone. I went away from my true nature, becoming a gentle, sensitive, shy person who hardly spoke and who faded into the background. The only person I addressed was my teacher. Kenji had become as diffident and unobtrusive as I had. Occasionally we conversed in hushed tones about calligraphy or the mainland style of painting. The Tohan men despised and discounted us.

Our stay in Tsuwano became like the memory of a dream to me. Had the sword fight really taken place? Had Kaede and I been caught and scorched by love? I hardly saw her for the next few days. The ladies lodged in separate houses and took their meals apart. It was not hard to act, as I told myself I must, as if she did not exist, but if I heard her voice my heart raced, and at night her image burned behind my eyes. Had I been bewitched?

The first night Abe ignored me, but on the second, after the evening meal, when wine had made him belligerent, he stared at me for a long time before remarking to Shigeru, "This boy—some relative, I suppose?"

"The son of a distant cousin of my mother," Shigeru replied. "He's the second oldest of a large family, all orphans now. My mother had always wanted to adopt him, and after her death I carried out her intention."

"And landed yourself with a milksop." Abe laughed.

"Well, sadly, maybe," Shigeru agreed. "But he has other talents that are useful. He is quick at calculating, and writing, and has some skill as an artist." His tone was patient, disappointed, as though I were an unwelcome burden to him, but I knew each comment like this served only to build up my character. I sat with eyes cast down, saying nothing.

Abe poured himself more wine and drank, eyeing me over the bowl's rim. His eyes were small and deep-set in a pockmarked, heavy-featured face. "Not much use in these times!"

"Surely we can expect peace, now that our two clans are moving towards alliance," Shigeru said quietly. "There may be a new flowering of the arts."

"Peace with the Otori maybe. They'll cave in without a fight. But now the Seishuu are causing trouble, stirred up by that traitor, Arai."

"Arai?" Shigeru questioned.

"A former vassal of Noguchi. From Kumamoto. His lands lie alongside your bride's family's. He's been raising fighting men all year. He'll have to be crushed before winter." Abe drank again. An expression of malicious humor crept into his face, making the mouth curve more cruelly. "Arai killed the man who allegedly tried to violate Lady Shirakawa, then took offense when Noguchi exiled him." His head swung towards me with the drunk's second sight. "I'll bet you've never killed a man, have you, boy?"

"No, Lord Abe," I replied. He laughed. I could sense the bully in him, close to the surface. I did not want to provoke him.

"How about you, old man?" He turned towards Kenji, who in his role of insignificant teacher had been drinking wine with delight. He seemed half intoxicated, but in fact was far less drunk than Abe.

"Although the sages teach us that the noble man may—indeed, should—avenge death," he said in a high-pitched, pious voice, "I have never had cause to take such extreme action. On the other hand, the Enlightened One teaches his followers to refrain from taking the life of any sentient being, which is why I partake only of vegetables." He drank with appreciation and refilled his bowl. "Luckily wine, brewed from rice, is included in that category."

"Don't you have any warriors in Hagi, that you travel with such companions?" Abe scoffed.

"I am supposed to be going to my wedding," Shigeru returned mildly. "Should I be more prepared for battle?"

"A man should always be prepared for battle," Abe replied, "especially when his bride has the reputation yours has. You're aware of it, I suppose?" He shook his massive head. "It would be like eating puffer fish. One bite might kill you. Doesn't it alarm you?"

"Should it?" Shigeru poured more wine and drank.

"Well, she's exquisite, I admit. It would be worth it!"

"Lady Shirakawa will be no danger to me," Shigeru said, and led Abe on to speak of his exploits during Iida's campaigns in the East. I listened to his boasting and tried to discern his weaknesses. I had already decided I was going to kill him.

The next day we came to Yamagata. It had been badly hit by the storm, with many dead and a huge loss of crops.

Nearly as big as Hagi, it had been the second city in the Otori fief, until it had been handed over to the Tohan. The castle had been rebuilt and given to one of Iida's vassals. But most of the townspeople still considered themselves Otori, and Lord Shigeru's presence was one more reason for unrest. Abe had hoped to be in Inuyama before the Festival of the Dead began, and was angry at being stuck in Yamagata. It was considered inauspicious to travel, except to temples and shrines, until the festival was over.

Shigeru was plunged into sadness, being for the first time at the place of Takeshi's death. "Every Tohan man I see, I ask myself: Were you one of them?" he confided in me late that night. "And I imagine they ask themselves why they are still unpunished, and despise me for letting them live. I feel like cutting them all down!"

I had never heard him express anything other than patience. "Then we would never get to Iida," I replied. "Every insult the Tohan heap on us will be avenged then."

"Your scholarly self is becoming very wise, Takeo," he said, his voice a little lighter. "Wise and self-controlled."

The next day he went with Abe to the castle to be received by the local lord. He came back sadder and more disturbed than ever. "The Tohan seek to avert unrest by blaming the Hidden for the disasters of the storms," he told me briefly. "A handful of wretched merchants and farmers were denounced and arrested. Some died under torture. Four are suspended from the castle walls. They've been there for three days."

"They're still alive?" I whispered, my skin crawling.

"They may last a week or more," Shigeru said. "In the meantime, the crows eat their living flesh."

Once I knew they were there, I could not stop hearing them: at times a quiet groaning, at other times a thin screaming, accompanied in daylight by the constant cawing and flapping of the crows. I heard it all that night and the following day, and then it was the first night of the Festival of the Dead.

The Tohan imposed a curfew on their towns, but the festival followed older traditions, and the curfew was lifted until midnight. As night fell we left the inn and joined the crowds of people going first to the temples and then to the river. All the stone lanterns that lined the approaches to the shrines were lit, and candles were set on the tombstones, the flickering lights throwing strange shadows that made bodies gaunt and faces skull-like. The throng moved steadily and silently as though the dead themselves had emerged from the earth. It was easy to get lost in it, easy to slip away from our watchful guards.

It was a warm, still night. I went with Shigeru to the riverbank, and we set lighted candles adrift in fragile little boats laden with offerings for the dead. The temple bells were tolling, and chanting and singing drifted across the slow, brown water. We watched the lights float away on the current, hoping the dead would be comforted and would leave the living in peace.

Except that I had no peace in my heart. I thought of my mother, my stepfather and my sisters, my long-dead father, the people of Mino. Lord Shigeru no doubt thought of his father, his brother. It seemed their ghosts would not leave us until they were avenged. All around us, people were setting their lit boats afloat, weeping and crying, and making my heart twist with useless sorrow that the world was how it was. The teaching of the Hidden, such as I remembered, came into my mind, but then I remembered that all those who had taught it to me were dead.

The candle flames burned for a long time, growing

smaller and smaller, until they looked like fireflies, and then like sparks, and then like the phantom lights you see when you gaze too long on flames. The moon was full, with the orange tinge of late summer. I dreaded going back to the inn, to the stuffy room where I would toss and turn all night and listen to the Hidden dying against the castle wall.

Bonfires had been lit along the riverbank, and now people began to dance, the haunting dance that welcomes the dead, lets them depart, and comforts the living. Drums were beating and music playing. It lifted my spirits a little and I got to my feet to watch. In the shadows of the willow trees I saw Kaede.

She was standing with Lady Maruyama, Sachie, and Shizuka. Shigeru stood up and strolled towards them. Lady Maruyama approached him, and they greeted each other in cool, formal language, exchanging sympathy for the dead and commenting on the journey. They turned, as was perfectly natural, to stand side by side and watch the dancing. But I felt I could hear the longing beneath their tone, and see it in their stance, and I was afraid for them. I knew they could dissemble—they had done so for years—but now they were entering a desperate endgame, and I feared they would throw away caution before the final move.

Kaede was now alone on the bank, apart from Shizuka. I seemed to arrive at her side without volition, as though I had been picked up by spirits and put down next to her. I managed to greet her politely but diffidently, thinking that if Abe spotted me, he would simply think I was suffering from calf-love for Shigeru's betrothed. I said something about the heat, but Kaede was trembling as though she were cold. We stood in silence for a few moments, then she asked in a low voice, "Who are you mourning, Lord Takeo?"

"My mother, my father." After a pause I went on, "There are so many dead."

"My mother is dying," she said. "I hoped I would see her again, but we have been so delayed on this journey, I fear I will be too late. I was seven years old when I was sent as a hostage. I have not seen my mother or my sisters for over half my life."

"And your father?"

"He is also a stranger to me."

"Will he be at your . . . ?" To my surprise my throat dried up, and I found I could not speak the word.

"My marriage?" she said, bitterly. "No, he will not be there." Her eyes had been fixed on the light-filled river. Now

45

she looked past me at the dancers, at the crowd watching them.

"They love each other," she said, as though speaking to herself. "That's why she hates me."

I knew I should not be there, I should not be talking to her, but I could not make myself move away. I tried to maintain my gentle, diffident, well-behaved character. "Marriages are made for reasons of duty and alliance. That does not mean they have to be unhappy. Lord Otori is a good man."

"I am tired of hearing that. I know he is a good man. I am only saying, he will never love me." I knew her eyes were on my face. "But I know," she went on, "that love is not for our class."

I was the one who was trembling now. I raised my head, and my eyes met hers.

"So why do I feel it?" she whispered.

I did not dare say anything. The words I wanted to say swelled up huge in my mouth. I could taste their sweetness and their power. Again I thought I would die if I did not possess her.

The drums pounded. The bonfires blazed. Shizuka spoke out of the darkness. "It's growing late, Lady Shirakawa."

"I am coming," Kaede said. "Good night, Lord Takeo."

I allowed myself one thing, to speak her name, as she had spoken mine. "Lady Kaede."

In the moment before she turned away, I saw her face come alight, brighter than the flames, brighter than the moon on the water.

· 2 ·

We followed the women slowly back to the town, and then went to our separate lodging houses. Somewhere on the way the Tohan guards caught up with us, and we had their escort to the inn door. They stayed outside and one of our own Otori men kept watch in the passageway.

"Tomorrow we will ride to Terayama," Shigeru said as we prepared for bed. "I must visit Takeshi's grave and pay my respects to the abbot, who was an old friend of my father's. I have some gifts for him from Hagi."

We had brought with us many gifts. The packhorses had been laden with them, along with our own baggage, clothes for the wedding, food for the journey. I did not think anything more of the wooden box that we would carry to Terayama, or what it might contain. I was restless with other longings, other concerns.

The room was as stuffy as I'd feared. I could not sleep. I heard the temple bells toll at midnight, and then all sounds faded away under the curfew, apart from the pitiful groans of the dying from the castle walls.

In the end I got up. I had no real plan in my head. I was just driven into action by sleeplessness. Both Kenji and Shigeru were asleep, and I could tell that the guard outside was dozing. I took the watertight box in which Kenji kept capsules of poison, and tied it inside my undergarment. I dressed in dark traveling clothes and took the short sword, thin garrotes, a pair of grapples, and a rope from their hiding place within the wooden chests. Each of these movements took a long time, as I had to execute them in complete silence, but time is different for the Tribe, slowing down or speeding up as we will it to. I was in no hurry, and I knew the two men in the room would not wake.

The guard stirred as I stepped past him. I went to the privy to relieve myself, and sent my second self back past him into the room. I waited in the shadows until he dozed again, then went invisible, scaled the roof from the inner courtyard, and dropped down into the street.

I could hear the Tohan guards at the gate of the inn, and I knew there would be patrols in the streets. With one part of my mind I was aware that what I was doing was danger-ous to the point of madness, but I could not help myself. Partly I wanted to test the skills Kenji had taught me before we got to Inuyama, but mostly I just wanted to silence the groans from the castle so that I could go to sleep.

I worked my way through the narrow streets, zigzagging towards the castle. A few houses still had lights behind the shutters, but most were already in darkness. I caught snatches of conversation as I went past: a man comforting a weeping woman, a child babbling as if in fever, a lullaby, a drunken argument. I came out onto the main road that led straight to the moat and the bridge. A canal ran alongside it, stocked against siege with carp. Mostly they slept, their scales shining faintly in the moonlight. Every now and then one would wake with a sudden flip and splash. I wondered if they dreamed.

I went from doorway to doorway, ears alert all the time for the tread of feet, the clink of steel. I was not particularly worried about the patrols: I knew I would hear them long before they heard me, and above that, I had the skills of invisibility and the second self. By the time I reached the end of the street and saw the waters of the moat under the moonlight, I had stopped thinking much at all, beyond a satisfaction deep within me that I was Kikuta and doing what I was born to do. Only the Tribe know this feeling.

On the town side of the moat there was a clump of willow trees, their heavy summer foliage falling right to the water. For defensive purposes they should have been cleared: Maybe some resident of the castle, the lord's wife or mother, loved their beauty. Under the moonlight their branches looked frozen. There was no wind at all. I slipped between them, crouched down, and looked at the castle for a long time.

It was bigger than the castles at either Tsuwano or Hagi, but the construction was similar. I could see the faint outline of the baskets against the white walls of the keep behind the second south gate. I had to swim the moat, scale the stone wall, get over the first gate and across the south bailey, climb the second gate and the keep, and climb down to the baskets from above.

I heard footsteps and shrank into the earth. A troop of

guards was approaching the bridge. Another patrol came from the castle, and they exchanged a few words.

"Any problems?"

"Just the usual curfew breakers."

"Terrible stink!"

"It'll be worse tomorrow. Hotter."

One group went into the town; the other walked over the bridge and up the steps to the gate. I heard the shout that challenged them, and their reply. The gate creaked as it was unbarred and opened. I heard it slam shut and the footsteps fade away.

From my position under the willows I could smell the stagnant waters of the moat, and beneath that another stench: of human corruption, of living bodies rotting slowly.

At the water's edge were flowering grasses and a few late irises. Frogs croaked and crickets shrilled. The warm air of the night caressed my face. Two swans, unbelievably white, drifted into the path of the moon.

I filled my lungs with air and slipped into the water, swimming close to the bottom and aiming slightly downstream so that I surfaced under the shadow of the bridge. The huge stones of the moat wall gave natural footholds; my main concern here was being seen against the pale stone. I could not maintain invisibility for more than a couple of minutes at a time. Time that had gone so slowly before now speeded up. I moved fast, going up the wall like a monkey. At the first gate I heard voices, the guards coming back from their circular patrol. I flattened myself against a drainpipe, went invisible, and used the sound of their steps to mask the grapple as I threw it up over the massive overhang of the wall.

I swung myself up and, staying on the tiled roof, ran around to the south bailey. The baskets with the dying men in them were almost directly over my head. One was calling over and over for water, one moaned wordlessly, and one was repeating the name of the secret god in a rapid monotone that made the hairs on the back of my neck stand up. The fourth was completely silent. The smell of blood, piss, and shit was terrible. I tried to close my nostrils to it, and my ears to the sounds. I looked at my hands in the moonlight.

I had to cross above the gatehouse. I could hear the guards within it, making tea and chatting. As the kettle clinked on the iron chain, I used the grapples to climb the keep to the parapet that the baskets were slung from.

They were suspended by ropes, about forty feet above

the ground, each one just large enough to hold a man forced down on his knees, head bent forward, arms tied behind his back. The ropes seemed strong enough to bear my weight, but when I tested one from the parapet, the basket lurched and the man within cried out sharply in fear. It seemed to shatter the night. I froze. He sobbed for a few minutes, then whispered again, "Water! Water!"

There was no answering sound apart from a dog barking far in the distance. The moon was close to the mountains, about to disappear behind them. The town lay sleeping, calm.

When the moon had set, I checked the hold of the grapple on the parapet, took out the poison capsules, and held them in my mouth. Then I climbed down the wall, using my own rope and feeling for each foothold on the stone.

At the first basket I took off my headband, still wet from the river, and could just reach through the weave to hold it to the man's face. I heard him suck and say something incoherent.

"I can't save you," I whispered, "but I have poison. It will give you a quick death."

He pressed his face to the mesh and opened his mouth for it.

The next man could not hear me, but I could reach the carotid artery where his head was slumped against the side of the basket, and so I silenced his groans with no pain to him.

I then had to climb again to the parapet to reposition my rope, for I could not reach the other baskets. My arms were aching, and I was all too aware of the flagstones of the yard below. When I reached the third man, the one who had been praying, he was alert, watching me with dark eyes. I murmured one of the prayers of the Hidden and held out the poison capsule.

He said, "It is forbidden."

"Let any sin be on me," I whispered. "You are innocent. You will be forgiven."

As I pushed the capsule into his mouth, with his tongue he traced the sign of the Hidden against my palm. I heard him pray, and then he went silent forever.

I could feel no pulse at the throat of the fourth, and thought he was already dead, but just to be sure I used the garrote, tightening it around his neck and holding it while I counted the minutes away under my breath.

I heard the first cock crow. As I climbed back to the parapet the silence of the night was profound. I had stilled the groans and the screams. I thought the contrasting quiet was sure to wake the guards. I could hear my own pulse beat crashing like a drum.

I went back the way I had come, not using the grapple, but dropping from the walls to the ground, moving even faster than before. Another cock crowed and a third answered. The town would soon be waking. Sweat was pouring from me, and the waters of the moat felt icy. My breath barely held for the swim back, and I surfaced well short of the willow trees, startling the swans. I breathed and dived again.

I came up on the bank and headed for the willows, meaning to sit there for a few moments to get my breath back. The sky was lightening. I was exhausted. I could feel my concentration and focus slipping. I could hardly believe what I had done.

To my horror I heard someone already there. It was not a soldier but some outcaste, I thought, a leather worker perhaps, judging by the smell of the tannery that clung to him. Before I could recover my strength enough to go invisible, he saw me, and in that flash of a look I realized he knew what I had done.

Now I shall have to kill again, I thought, sickened that this time it would not be release but murder. I could smell blood and death on my own hands. I decided to let him live, left my second self beneath the tree, and in an instant was on the other side of the street.

I listened for a moment, and heard the man speak to my image before it faded.

"Sir," he said hesitantly, "forgive me. I've been listening to my brother suffer for three days. Thank you. May the secret one be with you and bless you."

Then my second self vanished and he cried out in shock and amazement. "An angel!"

I could hear his rough breathing, almost sobbing, as I ran from doorway to doorway. I hoped the patrols did not catch up with him, hoped he would not speak of what he had seen, trusted that he was one of the Hidden, who take their secrets to the grave.

The wall around the inn was low enough to leap up. I went back to the privy and the cistern, where I spat out the remaining capsules, and washed my face and hands as if I had just risen. The guard was half awake when I passed him. He mumbled, "Is it day already?"

57

"An hour away, still," I replied.

"You look pale, Lord Takeo. Have you been unwell?"

"A touch of the gripes, that's all."

"This damn Tohan food," he muttered, and we both laughed.

"Will you have some tea?" he asked. "I'll wake the maids."

"Later. I'll try and sleep for a while."

I slid the door open and stepped into the room. The darkness was just giving way to gray. I could tell by his breathing that Kenji was awake.

"Where've you been?" he whispered.

"In the privy. I didn't feel well."

"Since midnight?" he said, incredulous.

I was pulling off my wet clothes and hiding the weapons under the mattress at the same time. "Not that long. You were asleep."

He reached out and felt my undergarment. "This is soaking! Have you been in the river?"

"I told you, I didn't feel well. Maybe I couldn't get to the privy in time."

Kenji thwacked me hard on the shoulder, and I heard Shigeru wake.

"What is it?" he whispered.

"Takeo's been out all night. I was worried about him."

"I couldn't sleep," I said. "I just went out for a while. I've done it before, in Hagi and Tsuwano."

"I know you have," Kenji said. "But that was Otori country. It's a lot more dangerous here."

"Well, I'm back now." I slipped under the quilt and pulled it over my head, and almost immediately fell into a sleep as deep and dreamless as death.

When I woke, it was to the sound of the crows. I had only slept for about three hours, but I felt rested and peaceful. I did not think about the previous night. Indeed, I had no clear memory of it, as though I had acted in a trance. It was one of those rare days of late summer when the sky is a clear light blue and the air soft and warm, with no stickiness. A maid came into the room with a tray of food and tea and, after bowing to the floor and pouring the tea, said quietly, "Lord Otori is waiting for you in the stables. He asks you to join him as soon as possible. And your teacher wishes you to bring drawing materials."

I nodded, my mouth full.

She said, "I will dry your clothes for you."

"Get them later," I told her, not wanting her to find the weapons, and when she left I jumped up, got dressed, and hid the grapples and the garrote in the false bottom of the traveling chest where Kenji had packed them. I took up the pouch with my brushes, and the lacquer box that contained the ink stone, and wrapped them in a carrying cloth. I put my sword in my belt, thought myself into being Takeo, the studious artist, and went out to the stable yard.

As I passed the kitchen I heard one of the maids whisper, "They all died in the night. People are saying an angel of Death came. . . ."

I walked on, my eyes lowered, adjusting my gait so that I seemed a little clumsy. The ladies were already on horseback. Shigeru stood in conversation with Abe, who I realized was to accompany us. A young Tohan man stood beside them, holding two horses. A groom held Shigeru's Kyu and my Raku.

"Come along, come along," Abe exclaimed when he saw me. "We can't wait all day while you laze in bed."

"Apologize to Lord Abe," Shigeru said with a sigh.

"I am very sorry; there is no excuse at all," I babbled, bowing low to Abe and to the ladies, trying not to look at Kaede. "I was studying late."

Then I turned to Kenji and said deferentially, "I have brought the drawing materials, sir."

"Yes, good," he replied. "You will see some fine works at Terayama, and may even copy them if we have time."

Shigeru and Abe mounted, and the groom brought Raku to me. My horse was pleased to see me: He dropped his nose to my shoulder and nuzzled me. I let the movement push me off balance, so that I stumbled slightly. I went to Raku's right side and pretended to find mounting somewhat of a problem.

"Let's hope his drawing skills are greater than his horse-manship," Abe said derisively.

"Unfortunately, they are nothing out of the ordinary." I did not think Kenji's annoyance with me was feigned.

I made no reply to either of them, just contented myself with studying Abe's thick neck as he rode in front of me, imagining how it would feel to tighten the garrote around it or to slide a knife into his solid flesh.

These dark thoughts occupied me until we were over the bridge and out of the town. Then the beauty of the day began to work its magic on me. The land was healing itself after the ravages of the storm. Morning-glory flowers had opened, brilliant blue, even where the vines were torn down in the mud. Kingfishers flashed across the river, and egrets and herons stood in the shallows. A dozen different dragonflies hovered about us, and orange-brown and yellow butterflies flew up from around the horses' feet.

On the flat land of the river plain we rode between bright green rice fields, the plants flattened by the storm but already pushing themselves upright again. Everywhere people were hard at work; even they seemed cheerful despite the storm's destruction all around them. They reminded me of the people of my village, their indomitable spirit in the face of disaster, their unshakable belief that no matter what might befall them, life was basically good and the world benign. I wondered how many more years of Tohan rule would it take to gouge that belief from their hearts.

The paddy fields gave way to terraced vegetable gardens, and then, as the path became steeper, to bamboo groves, closing around us with their dim, silver-green light. The bamboo in its turn gave way to pines and cedars, the thick needles underfoot muffling the horses' tread.

Around us stretched the impenetrable forest. Occasionally we passed pilgrims on the path, making the arduous journey to the holy mountain. We rode in single file, so conversation was difficult. I knew Kenji was longing to question me about the previous night, but I did not want to talk about it or even to think about it.

After nearly three hours we came to the small cluster of buildings around the outer gate of the temple. There was a lodging house here for visitors. The horses were taken away to be fed and watered, and we ate the midday meal, simple vegetable dishes prepared by the monks.

"I am a little tired," Lady Maruyama said when we had finished eating. "Lord Abe, will you stay here with Lady Shirakawa and myself while we rest for a while?"

He could not refuse, though he seemed reluctant to let Shigeru out of his sight.

Shigeru gave the wooden box to me, asking me to carry it up the hill, and I also took my own pack of brushes and ink. The young Tohan man came with us, scowling a little, as though he distrusted the whole excursion, but it must have seemed harmless enough, even to the suspicious. Shigeru could hardly pass by so close to Terayama without visiting his brother's grave, especially a year after his death and at the time of the Festival of the Dead.

We began to climb the steep stone steps. The temple was built on the side of the mountain, next to a shrine of great antiquity. The trees in the sacred grove must have been four or five hundred years old, their huge trunks rising up into the canopy, their gnarled roots clinging to the mossy ground like forest spirits. In the distance I could hear monks chanting and the boom of gongs and bells, and beneath these sounds the voice of the forest, the min-min, the splash of the water-fall, the wind in the cedars, birds calling. My high spirits at the beauty of the day gave way to another, deeper feeling; a sense of awe and expectancy, as if some great and wonderful secret were about to be revealed to me.

We came finally to the second gate, which led into another cluster of buildings, where pilgrims and other visitors stayed. Here we were asked to wait and given tea to drink. After a few moments two priests approached us. One was an old man, rather short and frail with age, but with bright eyes and an expression of great serenity. The other was much younger, stern-faced and muscular.

"You are very welcome here, Lord Otori," the old man said, making the Tohan man's face darken even more. "It was with great sorrow that we buried Lord Takeshi. You have come, of course, to visit the grave."

"Stay here with Muto Kenji," Shigeru said to the soldier, and he and I followed the old priest to the graveyard, where the tombstones stood in rows beneath the huge trees. Someone was burning wood, and the smoke drifted beneath the trunks, making blue rays out of the sunlight.

The three of us knelt in silence. After a few moments the younger priest came with candles and incense and passed them to Shigeru, who placed them before the stone. The sweet fragrance floated around us. The lamps burned steadily, since there was no wind, but their flames could hardly be seen in the brightness of the sun. Shigeru also took two objects from his sleeve—a black stone like the ones from the seashore around Hagi, and a straw horse such as a child might play with—and placed these on the grave.

I remembered the tears he had shed the first night I had met him. Now I understood his grief, but neither of us wept.

After a while the priest rose, touching Shigeru on the shoulder, and we followed him to the main building of this remote country temple. It was made of wood, cypress and cedar, which had faded over time to silver gray. It did not look large, but its central hall was perfectly proportioned, giving a sense of space and tranquillity, leading the gaze inwards to where the golden statue of the Enlightened One seemed to hover among the candle flames as if in Paradise.

We loosened our sandals and stepped up into the hall. Again the young monk brought incense, and we placed it at the golden feet of the statue. Kneeling to one side of us, he began to chant one of the sutras for the dead.

It was dim inside, and my eyes were dazzled by the candles, but I could hear the breathing of others within the temple, beyond the altar, and as my vision adjusted to the darkness I could see the shapes of monks sitting in silent meditation. I realized the hall was much bigger than I had at first thought, and there were many monks here, possibly hundreds.

Even though I was raised among the Hidden, my mother took me to the shrines and temples of our district, and I knew a little of the teachings of the Enlightened One. I thought now, as I had often thought before, that people when they pray look and sound the same. The peace of this place pierced my soul. What was I doing here, a killer, my heart bent on revenge?

When the ceremony was over we went back to join Kenji, who seemed to be deep in a one-sided discussion with the Tohan man about art and religion.

"We have a gift for the lord abbot," Shigeru said, picking up the box, which I had left with Kenji.

A twinkle appeared in the priest's eye. "I will take you to him."

"And the young men would like to see the paintings," Kenji said.

"Makoto will show them. Follow me, please, Lord Otori."

The Tohan man looked taken aback as Shigeru disappeared behind the altar with the old priest. He made as if to follow them, but Makoto seemed to block his path, without touching or threatening him.

"This way, young man!"

With a deliberate tread he somehow herded the three of us out of the temple and along a boardwalk to a smaller hall.

"The great painter Sesshu lived in this temple for ten years," he told us. "He designed the gardens and painted landscapes, animals, and birds. These wooden screens are his work."

"That is what it is to be an artist," Kenji said in his querulous teacher's voice.

"Yes, master," I replied. I did not have to pretend to be humble: I was genuinely awed by the work before our eyes. The black horse, the white cranes, seemed to have been caught and frozen in an instant of time by the consummate skill of the artist. You felt that at any moment the spell would be broken, the horse would stamp and rear, the cranes would see us and launch themselves into the sky. The painter had achieved what we would all like to do: capture time and make it stand still.

The screen closest to the door seemed to be bare. I peered at it, thinking the colors must have faded. Makoto said, "There were birds on it, but the legend goes that they were so lifelike, they flew away."

"You see how much you have to learn," Kenji told me. I thought he was rather overdoing it, but the Tohan man gave me a scornful glance and, after a cursory look at the paintings, went outside and sat down under a tree.

I took out the ink stone, and Makoto brought me some water. I prepared the ink and unfolded a roll of paper. I wanted to trace the master's hand and see if he could transfer, across the chasm of the years, what he had seen, into my brush.

Outside, the afternoon heat increased, shimmering, intensified by the crickets' shrilling. The trees cast great pools of inky shade. Inside the hall it was cooler, dim. Time slowed. I heard the Tohan man's breathing even as he fell asleep.

"The gardens are also Sesshu's work," Makoto said, and he and Kenji sat themselves down on the matting, their backs towards the paintings and me, looking out onto the rocks and trees. In the distance a waterfall murmured, and I could hear two wood doves cooing. From time to time Kenji made a comment or asked a question about the garden, and Makoto replied. Their conversation grew more desultory, until they also seemed to be dozing.

Left alone with my brush and paper, and the incomparable paintings, I felt the same focus and concentration steal over me that I'd felt the previous night, taking me into the same half-trancelike state. It saddened me a little that the skills of the Tribe should be so similar to the skills of art. A strong desire seized me to stay in this place for ten years like the great Sesshu, and draw and paint every day until my paintings came to life and flew away.

I made copies of the horse and the cranes, copies that

did not satisfy me at all, and then I painted the little bird from my mountain as I had seen it flying off at my approach, with a flash of white in its wings.

I was absorbed by the work. From far away I could hear Shigeru's voice, speaking to the old priest. I was not really listening: I assumed he was seeking some spiritual counsel from the old man, a private matter. But the words dropped into my hearing, and it slowly dawned on me that their talk was of something quite different: burdensome new taxes, curtailment of freedom, Iida's desire to destroy the temples, several thousand monks in remote monasteries, all trained as warriors and desiring to overthrow the Tohan and restore the lands to the Otori.

I grinned ruefully to myself. My concept of the temple as a place of peace, a sanctuary from war, was somewhat misplaced. The priests and the monks were as belligerent as we were, as bent on revenge.

I did one more copy of the horse, and felt happier with it. I had caught something of its fiery power. I felt that Sesshu's spirit had indeed touched me across time, and maybe had reminded me that when illusions are shattered by truth, talent is set free.

Then I heard another sound from far below that set my heart racing: Kaede's voice. The women and Abe were climbing the steps to the second gate.

I called quietly to Kenji, "The others are coming."

Makoto got swiftly to his feet and padded silently away. A few moments later the old priest and Lord Shigeru stepped into the hall, where I was putting the finishing strokes to the copy of the horse.

"Ah, Sesshu spoke to you!" the old priest said, smiling.

I gave the picture to Shigeru. He was sitting looking at it when the ladies and Abe joined us. The Tohan man woke and tried to pretend he had not been asleep. The talk was all of paintings and gardens. Lady Maruyama continued to pay special attention to Abe, asking his opinion and flattering him until even he became interested in the subject.

Kaede looked at the sketch of the bird. "May I have this?" she asked.

"If it pleases you, Lady Shirakawa," I replied. "I'm afraid it is very poor."

"It does please me," she said in a low voice. "It makes me think of freedom."

The ink had dried rapidly in the heat. I rolled the paper

and gave it to her, my fingers grazing hers for a moment. It was the first time we had touched. Neither of us said any more. The heat seemed more intense, the crickets more insistent. A wave of fatigue swept over me. I was dizzy with lack of sleep and emotion. My fingers had lost their assurance and trembled as I packed away the painting things.

"Let us walk in the garden," Shigeru said, and took the ladies outside. I felt the old priest's gaze on me.

"Come back to us," he said, "when all this is over. There will always be a place for you here."

I thought of all the turmoil and changes the temple had seen, the battles that raged around it. It seemed so tranquil: The trees stood as they had for hundreds of years, the Enlightened One sat among the candles with his serene smile. Yet, even in this place of peace, men were planning war. I could never withdraw into painting and planning gardens until Iida was dead.

"Will it ever be over?" I replied.

"Everything that has a beginning has an ending," he said.

I bowed to the ground before him, and he placed his palms together in a blessing.

Makoto walked out into the garden with me. He was

looking at me quizzically. "How much do you hear?" he said quietly.

I looked around. The Tohan men were with Shigeru at the top of the steps. "Can you hear what they are saying?"

He measured the space with his eye. "Only if they shout it."

"I hear every word. I can hear them in the eating house below. I can tell you how many people are gathered there."

It struck me then that it sounded like a multitude.

Makoto gave a short laugh, amazement mixed with appreciation. "Like a dog?"

"Yes, like a dog," I replied.

"Useful to your masters."

His words stayed with me. I was useful to my masters, to Lord Shigeru, to Kenji, to the Tribe. I had been born with dark talents I did not ask for, yet I could not resist honing and testing them, and they had brought me to the place I was now. Without them I would surely be dead. With them I was drawn every day further into this world of lies, secrecy, and revenge. I wondered how much of this Makoto would understand, and wished I could share my thoughts with him. I felt an instinctive liking for him—more than liking: trust. But

73

the shadows were lengthening; it was nearly the hour of the Rooster. We had to leave to get back to Yamagata before nightfall. There was no time to talk.

When we descended the steps there was indeed a huge crowd of people gathered outside the lodging house.

"Are they here for the festival?" I said to Makoto.

"Partly," he said, and then in an aside so no one else could hear him: "But mainly because they have heard Lord Otori is here. They haven't forgotten the way things were before Yaegahara. Nor have we here. . . .

"Farewell," he said as I mounted Raku. "We'll meet again."

On the mountain path, on the road, it was the same. Many people were out, and they all seemed to want to take a look with their own eyes at Lord Shigeru. There was something eerie about it, the silent people dropping to the ground as we rode past, then getting to their feet to stare after us, their faces somber, their eyes burning.

The Tohan men were furious, but there was nothing they could do. They rode some way ahead of me, but I could hear their whispered conversation as clearly as if they poured the words into my ears.

"What did Shigeru do at the temple?" Abe asked.

"Prayed, spoke to the priest. We were shown the works by Sesshu; the boy did some painting."

"I don't care what the boy did! Was Shigeru alone with the priest?"

"Only for a few minutes," the younger man lied.

Abe's horse plunged forward. He must have jerked on the bridle in anger.

"He's not plotting anything," the young man said airily. "It's all just what it seems. He's on his way to be married. I don't see why you're so worried. The three of them are harmless. Fools—cowards, even—but harmless."

"You're the fool if you think that," Abe growled. "Shigeru is a lot more dangerous than he seems. He's no coward, for a start. He has patience. And no one else in the Three Countries has this effect on the people!"

They rode in silence for a while, then Abe muttered, "Just one sign of treachery and we have him."

The words floated back to me through the perfect summer evening. By the time we reached the river it was dusk, a blue twilight lit by fireflies among the rushes. On the bank the bonfires were already blazing for the second night of the festival. The previous night had been grief-filled and subdued. Tonight the atmosphere was wilder, with an undercurrent of ferment and violence. The streets were crowded, the throng thickest along the edge of the moat. People were standing staring at the first gate of the castle.

As we rode past we could see the four heads displayed above the gate. The baskets had already been removed from the walls.

"They died quickly," Shigeru said to me. "They were lucky."

I did not reply. I was watching Lady Maruyama. She took one quick look at the heads and then turned away, her face pale but composed. I wondered what she was thinking, if she was praying.

The crowd rumbled and surged like a sorrowful beast at the slaughterhouse, alarmed by the stench of blood and death.

"Don't linger," Kenji said. "I'm going to listen to a little gossip here and there. I'll meet you back at the inn. Stay indoors." He called to one of the grooms, slid from his horse, gave the reins to the man, and disappeared into the crowd.

As we turned into the straight street I had run down the

night before, a contingent of Tohan men rode towards us
with drawn swords.

"Lord Abe!" called one of them. "We are to clear the
streets. The town is in turmoil. Get your guests inside and
put guards on the gates."

"What set this off?" Abe demanded.

"The criminals all died in the night. Some man claims
an angel came and delivered them!"

"Lord Otori's presence is not helping the situation," Abe
said bitterly as he urged us towards the inn. "We'll ride on
tomorrow."

"The festival is not over," Shigeru remarked. "Travel on
the third day will only bring bad luck."

"That can't be helped! The alternative could be worse."
He had drawn his sword and now it whistled through the air
as he slashed at the crowd. "Get down!" he yelled.

Alarmed by the noise, Raku plunged forward, and I
found myself riding knee to knee with Kaede. The horses
swung their heads towards each other, taking courage from
each other's presence. They trotted the length of the street in
perfect stride.

She said, looking forward, in a voice so quiet that no one

but I could hear it above the turmoil around us: "I wish we could be alone together. There are so many things I want to know about you. I don't even know who you really are. Why do you pretend to be less than you are? Why do you hide your deftness?"

I would have gladly ridden alongside her like that forever, but the street was too short, and I was afraid to answer her. I pushed my horse forward, as if indifferent to her, but my heart was pounding at her words. It was all I wanted: to be alone with her, to reveal my hidden self, to let go of all the secrets and deceptions, to lie with her, skin against skin.

Would it ever be possible? Only if Iida died.

When we came to the inn I went to oversee the care of the horses. The Otori men who had stayed behind greeted me with relief. They had been anxious for our safety.

"The town's alight," one said. "One false move and there'll be fighting on the streets."

"What have you heard?" I asked.

"Those Hidden the bastards were torturing. Someone got to them and killed them. Unbelievable! Then some man figures he saw an angel!"

"They know Lord Otori is here," another added. "They still consider themselves Otori. I reckon they've had enough of the Tohan."

"We could take this town if we had a hundred men," the first muttered.

"Don't say these things, even to yourselves, even to me," I warned them. "We don't have a hundred men. We are at the mercy of the Tohan. We are supposed to be the instruments of an alliance: We must be seen to be such. Lord Shigeru's life depends on it."

They went on grumbling while they unsaddled the horses and fed them. I could feel the fire starting to burn in them, the desire to wipe out old insults and settle old scores.

"If any one of you draws a sword against the Tohan, his life is forfeit to me!" I said angrily.

They were not deeply impressed. They might know more about me than Abe and his men, but still, to them I was just young Takeo, a bit studious, fond of painting, not bad with the sword stick now, but always too gentle, too soft. The idea that I would actually kill one of them made them grin.

I feared their recklessness. If fighting broke out I had no

doubt that the Tohan would seize the chance to charge Shigeru with treachery. Nothing must happen now that would prevent us getting unsuspected to Inuyama.

By the time I left the stables my head was aching fiercely. I felt as if it had been weeks since I'd slept. I went to the bath-house. The girl who had brought me tea that morning and had said she would dry my clothes was there. She scrubbed my back and massaged my temples, and would certainly have done more for me if I had not been so tired and my mind so full of Kaede. She left me soaking in the hot water, but as she withdrew she whispered, "The work was well done."

I'd been dozing off but her words made me snap awake. "What work?" I asked, but she was already gone. Uneasy, I got out of the tub and returned to the room, the headache still a dull pain across my forehead.

Kenji was back. I could hear him and Shigeru speaking in low voices. They broke off when I entered the room, both staring at me. I could see from their faces that they knew.

Kenji said, "How?"

I listened. The inn was quiet, the Tohan still out on the streets. I whispered, "Two with poison, one with the garrote, one with my hands."

He shook his head. "It's hard to believe. Within the castle walls? Alone?"

I said, "I can't remember much about it. I thought you would be angry with me."

"I am angry," he replied. "More than angry—furious. Of all the idiotic things to do. We should be burying you tonight, by all rights."

I braced myself for one of his blows. Instead he embraced me. "I must be getting fond of you," he said. "I don't want to lose you."

"I would not have thought it possible," Shigeru said. It seemed he could not help smiling. "Our plan may succeed after all!"

"People in the street are saying it must be Shintaro," Kenji remarked, "though no one knows who paid him or why."

"Shintaro is dead," I said.

"Well, not many people know that. Anyway, the general opinion is that this assassin is some sort of heavenly spirit."

"A man saw me, the brother of one of the dead. He saw my second self, and when it faded he thought it was an angel."

"As far as I can find out, he has no idea of your identity.

It was dark, he did not see you clearly. He truly thought it was an angel."

"But why did you do it, Takeo?" Shigeru asked. "Why take such a risk now?"

Again, I could hardly remember. "I don't know, I couldn't sleep. . . ."

"It's that softness he has," Kenji said. "It drives him to act from compassion, even when he kills."

"There's a girl here," I said. "She knows something. She took my wet clothes this morning, and just now she said—"

"She's one of us," Kenji interrupted me, and as soon as he said it I realized I'd known that she was from the Tribe. "Of course, the Tribe suspected at once. They know how Shintaro died. They know you are here with Lord Shigeru. No one can believe you did it without being detected, but they also know there is no one else who could have done it."

"Can it be kept a secret, though?" Shigeru asked.

"No one's going to give Takeo away to the Tohan, if that's what you mean. And they don't seem to suspect anything. Your acting's improving," he told me. "Even I believed you were no more than a well-meaning bumbler today."

Shigeru smiled again. Kenji went on, his voice unnaturally

casual, "The only thing is, Shigeru, I know your plans; I know Takeo has agreed to serve you in their execution. But after this episode, I don't believe the Tribe will allow Takeo to remain with you much longer. They are now certain to claim him."

"Another week is all we need," Shigeru whispered.

I felt the darkness rise like ink in my veins. I raised my eyes and looked Shigeru full in the face—something I still rarely dared to do. We smiled at each other, never closer than when we were agreed on assassination.

From the streets outside came sporadic shouts, cries, the pad of running men, the tramp of horses, the crackling of fires, rising to wailing and screaming. The Tohan were clearing the streets, imposing the curfew. After a while the noise abated and the quiet of the summer evening returned. The moon had risen, drenching the town in light. I heard horses come into the inn yard, and Abe's voice. A few moments later there was a soft tap on the door, and maids came in with trays of food. One of them was the girl who had spoken to me earlier. She stayed to serve us after the others had left, saying quietly to Kenji, "Lord Abe has returned, sir. There will be extra guards outside the rooms tonight. Lord Otori's men are to be replaced by Tohan."

"They won't like that," I said, recalling the men's unrest.

"It seems provocative," Shigeru murmured. "Are we under some suspicion?"

"Lord Abe is angry and alarmed by the level of violence in the town," the girl replied. "He says it is to protect you."

"Would you ask Lord Abe to be good enough to wait on me?"

The girl bowed and left. We ate, mostly in silence. Towards the end of the meal Shigeru began to speak of Sesshu and his paintings. He took out the scroll of the horse and unrolled it. "It's quite pleasing," he said. "A faithful copy, yet something of yourself in it. You could become quite an artist . . ."

He did not go on, but I was thinking the same thought: *in a different world, in a different life, in a country not governed by war . . .*

"The garden is very beautiful," Kenji observed. "Although it is small, to my mind it is more exquisite than the larger examples of Sesshu's work."

"I agree," Shigeru said. "Of course, the setting at Terayama is incomparable."

I could hear Abe's heavy tread approaching. As the

door slid open I was saying humbly, "Can you explain the placement of the rocks to me, sir?"

"Lord Abe," Shigeru said, "please come in." He called to the girl: "Bring fresh tea and wine."

Abe bowed somewhat perfunctorily and settled himself on the cushions. "I will not stay long: I have not yet eaten, and we must be on the road at first light."

"We were speaking of Sesshu," Shigeru said. The wine was brought and he poured a cup for Abe.

"A great artist," Abe agreed, drinking deeply. "I regret that in these troubled times, the artist is less important than the warrior." He threw a scornful look at me that convinced me my disguise was still safe. "The town is quiet now, but the situation is still grave. I feel my men will offer you greater protection."

"The warrior is indispensable," Shigeru said. "Which is why I prefer to have my own men around me."

In the silence that followed I saw clearly the difference between them. Abe was no more than a glorified baron. Shigeru was heir to an ancient clan. Despite his reluctance, Abe had to defer to him.

He pushed his lower lip out. "If that is Lord Otori's wish . . ." he conceded finally.

"It is." Shigeru smiled slightly and poured more wine.

After Abe had left, the lord said, "Takeo, watch with the guards tonight. Impress on them that if there are any disturbances, I won't hesitate to hand them over to Abe for punishment. I fear a premature uprising. We are so close now to our aim."

It was an aim that I clung to single-mindedly. I gave no further thought to Kenji's statement that the Tribe would claim me. I concentrated solely on Iida Sadamu, in his lair in Inuyama. I would get to him across the nightingale floor. And I would kill him. Even the thought of Kaede only served to intensify my resolve. I didn't need to be an Ichiro to work out that if Iida died before Kaede's marriage, she would be set free to marry me.

· 3 ·

We were roused early in the morning and were on the road a little after daybreak. The clearness of the day before had disappeared; the air was heavy and sticky. Clouds had formed in the night and rain threatened.

People had been forbidden to gather in the streets, and the Tohan enforced the ruling with their swords, cutting down a night-soil collector who dared to stop and stare at our procession and beating to death an old woman who did not get out of the way in time.

It was inauspicious enough to be traveling on the third day of the Festival of the Dead. These acts of cruelty and bloodshed seemed added ill omens for our journey.

LIAN HEARN

The ladies were carried in palanquins, so I saw nothing of Kaede until we stopped for the midday meal. I did not speak to her, but I was shocked by her appearance. She was so pale, her skin seemed transparent, and her eyes were dark-ringed. My heart twisted. The more frail she became, it seemed the more hopelessly I loved her.

Shigeru spoke to Shizuka about her, concerned by her pallor. She replied that the movement of the palanquin did not agree with Kaede—it was nothing more than that—but her eyes flickered towards me and I thought I understood their message.

We were a silent group, each wrapped up in our own thoughts. The men were tense and irritable. The heat was oppressive. Only Shigeru seemed at ease, his conversation as light and carefree as if he were truly going to celebrate a longed-for wedding. I knew the Tohan despised him for it, but I thought it one of the greatest displays of courage I had seen.

The farther east we went, the less damage from the storms we encountered. The roads improved as we approached the capital, and each day we covered more miles. On the afternoon of the fifth day we arrived at Inuyama.

88

Iida had made this eastern city his capital after his success at Yaegahara, and had begun building the massive castle then. It dominated the town with its black walls and white crenellations, its roofs that looked as if they had been flung up into the sky like cloths. As we rode towards it I found myself studying the fortifications, measuring the height of the gates and the walls, looking for footholds. . . . Here I will go invisible, here I will need grapples. . . .

I had not imagined the town would be so large, that there would be so many warriors on guard in the castle and housed around it.

Abe reined his horse back so he was alongside me. I'd become a favorite butt for his jokes and bullying humor. "This is what power looks like, boy. You get it by being a warrior. Makes your work with the brush look pretty feeble, eh?"

I didn't mind what Abe thought of me, as long as he never suspected the truth. "It's the most impressive place I've ever seen, Lord Abe. I wish I could study it closely, its architecture, its works of art."

"I'm sure that can be arranged," he said, ready enough to be patronizing now that he was safely back in his own city.

"Sesshu's name still lives among us," I remarked, "while the warriors of his age have all been forgotten."

He burst out laughing. "But you're no Sesshu, are you?"

His contempt made the blood rise to his face, but I meekly agreed with him. He knew nothing about me: It was the only comfort I had.

We were escorted to a residence close to the castle moat. It was spacious and beautiful. All the appearances suggested that Iida was committed to the marriage and to the alliance with the Otori. Certainly no fault could be found with the attention and honor paid to Shigeru. The ladies were carried to the castle itself, where they would stay at Iida's own residence, with the women of his household. Lady Maruyama's daughter lived there.

I did not see Kaede's face, but as she was carried away she let her hand appear briefly through the curtain of the palanquin. In it she held the scroll I had given her, the painting of my little mountain bird that she said made her think of freedom.

A soft evening rain was beginning to fall, blurring the outlines of the castle, glistening on the tiles and the cobblestones. Two geese flew overhead with a steady beating of wings. As they disappeared from sight I could still hear their mournful cry.

Abe returned later to the residence with wedding gifts and effusive messages of welcome from Lord Iida. I reminded him of his promise to show me the castle, pestering him and putting up with his banter, until he agreed to arrange it for the following day.

Kenji and I went with him in the morning, and I dutifully listened and sketched while first Abe and then, when he grew bored, one of his retainers took us around the castle. My hand drew trees, gardens, and views, while eye and brain absorbed the layout of the castle, the distance from the main gate to the second gate (the Diamond Gate, they called it), from the Diamond Gate to the inner bailey, from the inner bailey to the residence. The river flowed along the eastern side; all four sides were moated. And while I drew I listened, placed the guards, both seen and hidden, and counted them.

The castle was full of people: warriors and foot soldiers, blacksmiths, fletchers and armorers, grooms, cooks, maids, servants of all kinds. I wondered where they all went at night, and if it ever became quiet.

The retainer was more talkative than Abe, keen to boast

about Iida, and naively impressed by my drawing. I sketched him quickly and gave him the scroll. In those days few portraits were made, and he held it as if it were a magic talisman. After that he showed us more than he should have, including the hidden chambers where guards were always stationed, the false windows of the watchtowers, and the route the patrols took throughout the night.

Kenji said very little, beyond criticizing my drawing and correcting a brushstroke now and then. I wondered if he was planning to come with me when I went into the castle at night. One moment I thought I could do nothing without his help; the next I knew I wanted to be alone.

We came finally to the central keep and were taken inside, introduced to the captain of the guard, and allowed to climb the steep wooden steps to the highest floor. The massive pillars that held up the main tower were at least seventy feet in height. I imagined them as trees in the forest, how vast their canopy would be, how dense and dark their shade. The crossbeams still held the twists they had grown with, as though they longed to spring upwards and be living trees again. I felt the castle's power as though it were a sentient being drawn up against me.

From the top platform, under the curious eyes of the midday guards, we could see out over the whole city. To the north rose the mountains I had crossed with Shigeru, and beyond them the plain of Yaegahara. To the southeast lay my birthplace, Mino. The air was misty and still, with hardly a breath of wind. Despite the heavy stone walls and the cool, dark wood, it was stiflingly hot. The guards' faces shone with sweat, their armor heavy and uncomfortable.

The southern windows of the main keep looked down onto the second, lower keep, which Iida had transformed into his residence. It was built above a huge fortification wall that rose almost directly from the moat. Beyond the moat, on the eastern side, was a strip of marshland, about a hundred yards or so in width, and then the river, flowing deep and strong, swollen by the storms. Above the fortification wall ran a row of small windows, but the doors of the residence were all on the western side. Gracefully sloping roofs covered the verandas and gave onto a small garden, surrounded by the walls of the second bailey. It would have been hidden from the eye at ground level, but here we could peer down into it as eagles might.

On the opposite side the northwest bailey housed the kitchens and other offices.

My eyes kept going from one side of Iida's palace to the other. The western side was so beautiful, almost gentle, the eastern side brutal in its austerity and power, and the brutality was increased by the iron rings set in the walls below the lookout windows. These, the guards told us, were used to hang Iida's enemies from, the victims' suffering deepening and enhancing his enjoyment of his power and splendor.

As we descended the steps again I could hear them mocking us, making the jokes I'd learned the Tohan always made at Otori expense: that they prefer boys to girls in bed, they'd rather eat a good meal than have a decent fight, that they were seriously weakened by their addiction to hot springs, which they always pissed in. Their raucous laughter floated after us. Embarrassed, our companion muttered an apology.

Assuring him we had taken no offense, I stood for a moment in the gateway of the inner bailey, ostensibly smitten by the beauty of the morning-glory flowers that straggled over the stone walls of the kitchens. I could hear all the usual kitchen sounds: the hiss of boiling water, the clatter of steel knives, a steady pounding as someone made rice cakes, the shouts of the cooks and the servant girls' high-pitched chatter. But beneath all that, from the other direction, from within the garden wall, there was something else reaching into my ears.

After a moment I realized what it was: the tread of people coming and going across Iida's nightingale floor.

"Can you hear that strange noise?" I said innocently to Kenji.

He frowned. "What can it be?"

Our companion laughed. "That's the nightingale floor."

"The nightingale floor?" we questioned together.

"It's a floor that sings. Nothing can cross it, not even a cat, without the floor chirping like a bird."

"It sounds like magic," I said.

"Maybe it is," the man replied, laughing at my credulity. "Whatever it is, his lordship sleeps better at night for its protection."

"What a marvelous thing! I'd love to see it," I said.

The man, still smiling, obligingly led us round the bailey to the southern side where the gate to the garden stood open. The gate was not high, but it had a massive overhang, and the steps through it were set on a steep angle so that they could be defended by one man. We looked through the gate to the building beyond. The wooden shutters were all open. I could see the massive gleaming floor that ran the whole length of the building.

A procession of maids bringing trays of food, for it was almost midday, stepped out of their sandals and onto the floor. I listened to its song, and my heart failed me. I recalled running so lightly and silently across the floor around the house in Hagi. This floor was four times its size, its song infinitely more complex. There would be no opportunity to practice. I would have one chance alone to outwit it.

I stayed as long as I plausibly could, exclaiming and admiring while trying to map every sound, and from time to time, remembering that Kaede was somewhere within that building, straining my ears in vain to hear her voice.

Eventually Kenji said, "Come along, come along! My stomach is empty. Lord Takeo will be able to see the floor again tomorrow when he accompanies Lord Otori."

"Do we come to the castle again tomorrow?"

"Lord Otori will wait on Lord Iida in the afternoon," Kenji said. "I suppose Lord Takeo will accompany him."

"How thrilling," I replied, but my heart was as heavy as stone at the prospect.

When we returned to our lodging house, Lord Shigeru

was looking at wedding robes. They were spread out over the matting, sumptuous, brightly colored, embroidered with all the symbols of good fortune and longevity: plum blossoms, white cranes, turtles.

"My uncles have sent these for me," he said. "What do you think of their graciousness, Takeo?"

"It is extreme," I replied, sickened by their duplicity.

"Which should I wear, in your opinion?" He took up the plum-blossom robe and the man who had brought the garments helped him put it on.

"That one is fine," Kenji said. "Now let's eat."

Lord Shigeru, however, lingered for a moment, passing his hands over the fine fabric, admiring the delicate intricacy of the embroidery. He did not speak, but I thought I saw something in his face: regret, perhaps, for the wedding that would never take place, and maybe, when I recall it now, pre-monition of his own fate.

"I will wear this one," he said, taking it off and handing it to the man.

"It is indeed becoming," the man murmured. "But few men are as handsome as Lord Otori."

Shigeru smiled his openhearted smile but made no other

response, nor did he speak much during the meal. We were all silent, too tense to speak of trivial matters, and too aware of possible spies to speak of anything else.

I was tired but restless. The afternoon heat kept me inside. Although the doors were all opened wide onto the garden, not a breath of air came into the rooms. I dozed, trying to recall the song of the nightingale floor. The sounds of the garden, the insects' droning, the waterfall's splash, washed over me, half waking me, making me think I was back in the house in Hagi.

Towards evening, rain began to fall again and it became a little cooler. Kenji and Shigeru were engrossed in a game of Go, Kenji being the black player. I must have fallen completely asleep, for I was awakened by a tap on the door and heard one of the maids tell Kenji a messenger had come for him.

He nodded, made his move, and got up to leave the room. Shigeru watched him go, then studied the board, as though absorbed only in the problems of the game. I stood, too, and looked at the layout of the pieces. I had watched the two of them play many times, and always Shigeru proved the stronger player, but this time I could tell the white pieces were under threat.

I went to the cistern and splashed water on my face and hands. Then, feeling trapped and suffocated inside, I crossed the courtyard to the main door of the lodging house and stepped out into the street.

Kenji stood on the opposite side of the road, talking to a young man who was dressed in the running clothes of a messenger. Before I could catch what they were saying, he spotted me, clapped the young man on the shoulder, and bade him farewell. He crossed the street towards me, dissembling, looking like my harmless old teacher. But he would not look me in the eye, and in the moment before he'd seen me I felt that the true Muto Kenji had been revealed, as it had been once before: the man beneath all the disguises, as ruthless as Jato.

They continued to play Go until late into the night. I could not bear to watch the slow annihilation of the white player, but I could not sleep, either, my mind full of what lay ahead of me, and plagued, too, by suspicions of Kenji. The next morning he went out early, and while he was away Shizuka came, bringing wedding gifts from Lady Maruyama. Concealed in the wrapping were two small scrolls. One was a letter, which Shizuka passed to Lord Shigeru.

He read it, his face closed and lined with fatigue. He did not tell us what was in it, but folded it and put it in the sleeve of his robe. He took the other scroll and, after glancing at it, passed it to me. The words were cryptic, but after a few moments I grasped their meaning. It was a description of the interior of the residence, and clearly showed where Iida slept.

"Better to burn them, Lord Otori," Shizuka whispered.

"I will. What other news?"

"May I come closer?" she asked, and spoke into his ear so quietly that only he and I could hear. "Arai is sweeping through the southwest. He has defeated the Noguchi and is within reach of Inuyama."

"Iida knows this?"

"If not, he soon will. He has more spies than we do."

"And Terayama? Have you heard from there?"

"They are confident they can take Yamagata without a struggle, once Iida—"

Shigeru held up a hand, but she had already stopped speaking.

"Tonight, then," he said briefly.

"Lord Otori." Shizuka bowed.

"Is Lady Shirakawa well?" he said in a normal voice, moving away from her.

"I wish she were better," Shizuka replied quietly. "She does not eat or sleep."

My heart had stopped beating for a moment when Shigeru had said tonight. Then it had taken on a rapid but measured rate, sending the blood powering through my veins. I looked once more at the plan in my hand, writing its message into my brain. The thought of Kaede, her pale face, the fragile bones of her wrists, the black mass of her hair, made my heart falter again. I stood up and went to the door to hide my emotion.

"I deeply regret the harm I am doing her," Shigeru said.

"She fears to bring harm to you," Shizuka replied, and added in a low voice, "among all her other fears. I must return to her. I am afraid to leave her alone."

"What do you mean?" I exclaimed, making them both look at me.

Shizuka hesitated. "She often speaks of death," she said finally.

I wanted to send some message to Kaede. I wanted to run to the castle and pluck her out of it—take her away somewhere where we would be safe. But I knew there was no such place, and never would be, until all this was over. . . .

I also wanted to ask Shizuka about Kenji—what he was up to, what the Tribe had in mind—but maids came bringing the midday meal, and there was no further opportunity to speak in private before she left.

We spoke briefly of the arrangements for the afternoon's visit while we ate. Afterwards, Shigeru wrote letters while I studied my sketches of the castle. I was aware of his gaze often on me, and felt there were many things he still wished to say to me, but he did not say them. I sat quietly on the floor, looking out onto the garden, letting my breathing slow, retreating into the dark silent self that dwelled within me, setting it loose so that it took over every muscle, sinew, and nerve. My hearing seemed sharper than ever. I could hear the whole town, its cacophony of human and animal life, joy, desire, pain, grief. I longed for silence, to be free of it all. I longed for night to come.

Kenji returned, saying nothing of where he had been. He watched silently as we dressed ourselves in formal robes with the Otori crest on the back. He spoke once to suggest that it might be wiser for me not to go to the castle, but Shigeru pointed out I would draw more attention to myself if I stayed behind. He did not add that I needed to see the castle one more time. I was also aware that I needed to see Iida again. The only image I had of him was of the terrifying figure I had seen in Mino a year ago: the black armor, the antlered helmet, the sword that had so nearly ended my life. So huge and powerful had this image become in my mind that to see him in the flesh, out of armor, was a shock.

We rode with all twenty of the Otori men. They waited in the first bailey with the horses while Shigeru and I went on with Abe. As we stepped out of our sandals onto the nightingale floor, I held my breath, listening for the birdsong beneath my feet. The residence was dazzlingly decorated in the modern style, the paintings so exquisite that they almost distracted me from my dark purpose. They were not quiet and restrained, like the Sesshus at Terayama, but gilded and flamboyant, full of life and power. In the antechamber, where we waited for over half an hour, the doors and screens were decorated with cranes in snowy willow trees. Shigeru admired them, and under Abe's sardonic eye we spoke in low voices of painting and of the artist.

"To my mind, these are far superior to Sesshu," the

Tohan lord said. "The colors are richer and brighter, and the scale is more ambitious."

Shigeru murmured something that was neither agreement nor disagreement. I said nothing. A few moments later an elderly man came in, bowed to the floor, and spoke to Abe. "Lord Iida is ready to receive his guests."

We rose and stepped out again onto the nightingale floor, following Abe to the Great Hall. Here Lord Shigeru knelt at the entrance, and I imitated him. Abe gestured to us to step inside, where we knelt again, bowing right to the ground. I caught a glimpse of Iida Sadamu sitting at the far end of the hall on a raised platform, his cream and gold robes spread out around him, a red and gold fan in his right hand, a small black formal hat on his head. He was smaller than I remembered but no less imposing. He seemed eight or ten years older than Shigeru and was about a head shorter. His features were ordinary, apart from the fine shaped eyes that betrayed his fierce intelligence. He was not a handsome man, but he had a powerful, compelling presence. My old terror leaped fully awake inside me.

There were about twenty retainers in the room, all prostrate on the floor. Only Iida and the little page boy on his left sat upright. There was a long silence. It was approaching the hour of the Monkey. There were no doors open, and the heat was oppressive. Beneath the perfumed robes lay the rank smell of male sweat. Out of the corner of my eye I could see the lines of concealed closets, and from them I heard the breathing of the hidden guards, the faint creak as they shifted position. My mouth was dry.

Lord Iida spoke at last. "Welcome, Lord Otori. This is a happy occasion: a marriage, an alliance."

His voice was rough and perfunctory, making the polite forms of speech sound incongruous in his mouth.

Shigeru raised his head and sat unhurriedly. He replied equally formally, conveyed greetings from his uncles and the entire Otori clan. "I am happy that I may be of service to two great houses."

It was a subtle reminder to Iida that they were of equal rank, by birth and blood.

Iida smiled entirely mirthlessly and replied, "Yes, we must have peace between us. We do not want to see a repeat of Yaegahara."

Shigeru inclined his head. "What is past is past."

I was still on the floor, but I could see his face in profile.

His gaze was clear and straightforward, his features steady and cheerful. No one would guess that he was anything other than what he appeared: a young bridegroom, grateful for the favor of an older lord.

They spoke for a while, exchanging pleasantries. Then tea was brought and served to the two of them.

"The young man is your adopted son, I hear," Iida said as the tea was poured. "He may drink with us."

I had to sit up then, although I would have preferred not to. I bowed again to Iida and shuffled forward on my knees, willing my fingers not to tremble as I took the bowl. I could feel his gaze on me, but I did not dare meet his eyes, so I had no way of knowing if he recognized me as the boy who had burned his horse's flank and landed him on the ground in Mino.

I studied the tea bowl. Its glaze was a gleaming iron gray, filled with red lights, such as I had never seen before.

"He is a distant cousin of my late mother's," Lord Shigeru was explaining. "It was her desire that he be adopted into our family, and after her death I carried out her wishes."

"His name?" Iida's eyes did not leave my face as he drank noisily from his bowl.

"He has taken the name of Otori," Shigeru replied. "We call him Takeo."

He did not say after my brother, but I felt Takeshi's name hang in the air, as though his ghost had drifted into the hall.

Iida grunted. Despite the heat in the room, the atmosphere became chillier and more dangerous. I knew Shigeru was aware of it. I felt his body tense, though his face was still smiling. Beneath the pleasantries lay years of mutual dislike, compounded by the legacy of Yaegahara, Iida's jealousy, and Shigeru's grief and his desire for revenge.

I tried to become Takeo, the studious artist, introverted and clumsy, gazing in confusion at the ground.

"He has been with you how long?"

"About a year," Shigeru replied.

"There is a certain family resemblance," Iida said. "Ando, would you not agree?"

He was addressing one of the retainers who knelt sideways to us. The man raised his head and looked at me. Our eyes met, and I knew him at once. I recognized the long, wolfish face with its high, pale brow and deep-set eyes. His right side was hidden from me, but I did not need to see it to know that his right arm was missing, lopped off by Jato in Otori Shigeru's hand.

"A very strong resemblance," the man, Ando, said. "I thought that the first time I saw the young lord." He paused, and then added: "In Hagi."

I bowed humbly to him. "Forgive me, Lord Ando, I did not think we had had the pleasure of meeting."

"No, we did not meet," he agreed. "I merely saw you with Lord Otori, and thought how much you resembled . . . the family."

"He is, after all, a relative," Shigeru said, sounding not in the least perturbed by these cat-and-mouse exchanges. I was no longer in any doubt. Iida and Ando knew exactly who I was. They knew it was Shigeru who had rescued me. I fully expected them to order our arrest immediately, or to have the guards kill us where we sat, among the tea utensils.

Shigeru moved very slightly, and I knew he was prepared to leap to his feet, sword in hand, if it came to that. But he would not throw away the months of preparation lightly. The tension mounted in the room as the silence deepened.

Iida's lips curved in a smile. I could sense the pleasure he took in the situation. He would not go for the kill yet: He would toy with us a little longer. There was nowhere we could escape to, deep in Tohan territory, constantly under watch, with only twenty men. I had no doubt he planned to eliminate both of us, but he was going to savor the delight of having his old enemy in his power.

He moved on to discuss the wedding. Beneath the cursory politeness I could hear contempt and jealousy. "Lady Shirakawa has been a ward of Lord Noguchi, my oldest and most trusted ally."

He said nothing of Noguchi's defeat by Arai. Had he not heard of it, or did he think we did not yet know?

"Lord Iida does me great honor," Shigeru replied.

"Well, it was time we made peace with the Otori." Iida paused for a while and then said, "She's a beautiful girl. Her reputation has been unfortunate. I hope this does not alarm you."

There was the slightest ripple from the retainers—not quite laughter, just an easing of facial muscles into knowing smiles.

"I believe her reputation is unwarranted," Shigeru replied evenly. "And while I am here as Lord Iida's guest, I am in no way alarmed."

Iida's smile had faded and he was scowling. I guessed he was eaten up by jealousy. Politeness and his own self-esteem

109

should have prevented him from what he said next, but they did not. "There are rumors about you," he said bluntly.

Shigeru raised his eyebrows, saying nothing.

"A long-standing attachment, a secret marriage," Iida began to bluster.

"Lord Iida astonishes me," Shigeru replied coolly. "I am not young. It is natural I should have known many women."

Iida regained control of himself and grunted a reply, but his eyes burned with malevolence. We were dismissed with perfunctory courtesy, Iida saying no more than "I look forward to our meeting in three days' time, at the marriage ceremony."

When we rejoined the men, they were tense and bad-tempered, having had to put up with the taunts and threats of the Tohan. Neither Shigeru nor I said anything as we rode down the stepped street and through the first gate. I was absorbed in memorizing as much as I could of the castle layout, and my heart was smoldering with hatred and rage against Iida. I would kill him, for revenge for the past, for his insolent treatment of Lord Otori—and because if I did not kill him that night, he would kill us both.

The sun was a watery orb in the West as we rode back to the lodging house, where Kenji awaited us. There was a slight smell of burning in the room. He had destroyed the messages from Lady Maruyama while we were away. He studied our faces.

"Takeo was recognized?" he said.

Shigeru was taking off the formal robes. "I need a bath," he said, and smiled as if releasing himself a little from the iron self-control he had been exerting. "Can we speak freely, Takeo?"

From the kitchens came the sounds of the servants preparing the evening meal. Steps crossed the walkway from time to time, but the garden was empty. I could hear the guards at the main gate. I heard a girl approach them with bowls of rice and soup.

"If we whisper," I replied.

"We must speak quickly. Come close, Kenji. Yes, he was recognized. Iida is full of suspicions and fears. He will strike at any moment."

Kenji said, "I'll take him away at once. I can hide him within the city."

"No!" I said. "Tonight I go to the castle."

"It will be our only chance," Shigeru whispered. "We must strike first."

Kenji looked at each of us. He sighed deeply. "Then I will come with you."

"You've been a good friend to me," Shigeru said quietly. "You do not have to risk your life."

"It's not for you, Shigeru. It's to keep an eye on Takeo," Kenji replied. To me he said, "You'd better look at the walls and the moat again, before curfew. I'll walk down with you. Bring your drawing materials. There will be an interesting play of light on the water."

I gathered my things together and we left. But at the door, just before he stepped outside, Kenji surprised me by turning again to Shigeru and bowing deeply. "Lord Otori," he said. I thought he was being ironic; only later did I realize it was a farewell.

I made no farewells beyond the usual bow, which Shigeru acknowledged. The evening light from the garden was behind him and I could not see his face.

❧

The cloud cover had thickened. It was damp but not raining, a little cooler now the sun had set, but still heavy and muggy. The streets were filled with people taking advantage of the hour between sunset and curfew. They kept bumping into me, making me anxious and uneasy. I saw spies and assassins everywhere. The meeting with Iida had unnerved me, turning me once again into Tomasu, into the terrified boy who had fled from the ruins of Mino. Did I really think I could climb into Inuyama Castle and assassinate the powerful lord I had just seen, who knew I was one of the Hidden, the only one from my village to escape him before? I might pretend to be Lord Otori Takeo, or Kikuta—one of the Tribe—but the truth was, I was neither. I was one of the Hidden, one of the hunted.

We walked westwards, along the southern side of the castle. As it grew dark I was thankful that there would be no moon and no stars. Torches flared from the castle gate, and the shops were lit by candles and oil lamps. There was a smell of sesame and soy, rice wine and grilling fish. Despite everything, I was hungry. I thought to stop and buy something, but Kenji suggested going a little farther. The street became darker and emptier. I could hear some wheeled vehicle rumbling over cobblestones, and then the sounds of a flute. There was something unspeakably eerie about it. The hairs on the back of my neck stood up in warning.

"Let's go back," I said, and at that moment a small procession emerged from an alley in front of us. I took them for street performers of some sort. An old man wheeled a cart with decorations and pictures on it. A girl was playing the flute, but she let it fall when she saw us. Two young men came out of the shadows holding tops, one spinning, one flying. In the half-light they seemed magical, possessed by spirits. I stopped. Kenji stood right behind me. Another girl stepped towards us, saying, "Come and look, lord."

I recognized her voice, but it was a couple of moments before I placed her. Then I jumped backwards, evading Kenji and leaving my second self by the cart. It was the girl from the inn at Yamagata, the girl of whom Kenji had said, "She's one of us."

To my surprise one of the young men followed me, taking no notice of my image. I went invisible, but he guessed where I was. I knew for certain then. These were Tribe, come to claim me, as Kenji had said, had known they would. I dropped to the ground, rolled, slid beneath the cart, but my teacher was on the other side. I tried to bite his hand, but his other one came up to my jaw, forcing it away. I kicked him instead, went limp in his grasp, tried to slide through his fingers, but all the tricks I knew he had taught me.

"Be quiet, Takeo," he hissed. "Stop struggling. No one's going to hurt you."

"All right," I said, and went still. He loosened his grip and in that moment I got away from him. I pulled my knife from my sash. But the five of them were fighting in earnest now. One of the young men feinted at me, making me back up to the cart. I slashed out at him and felt the knife strike bone. Then I cut one of the girls. The other had gone invisible, and I felt her drop like a monkey from the top of the cart, her legs around my shoulders, one hand over my mouth, the other at my neck. I knew of course the place she was going for, and twisted violently, losing my balance. The man I'd cut got my wrist, and I felt it bend backwards until I lost my grip on the knife. The girl and I fell together to the ground. Her hands were still at my throat.

Just before I lost consciousness I clearly saw Shigeru sitting in the room, waiting for us to return. I tried to scream in outrage at the enormity of the betrayal, but my mouth was covered, and even my ears could hear nothing.

· 4 ·

It was early evening, on the third day after her arrival at Inuyama. Since the moment the swaying palanquin had carried her into the castle, Kaede's spirits had fallen lower and lower. Even more than Noguchi, Inuyama was oppressive and full of terror. The women of the household were subdued and grief-stricken, still mourning their lady, Iida's wife, who had died in the early summer. Kaede had only seen their lord briefly, but it was impossible not to be aware of his presence. He dominated the residence, and everyone moved in fear of his moods and rages. No one spoke openly. Congratulations were mouthed to her by women with tired voices and empty eyes, and they prepared her wedding robes with listless hands. She felt doom settle over her.

Lady Maruyama, after her initial joy at seeing her daughter, was preoccupied and tense. Several times she seemed inclined to take Kaede into her confidence, but they were rarely alone for long. Kaede spent the hours trying to recall all the events of the journey, trying to make some sense out of the undercurrents that swirled around her, but she realized she knew nothing. Nothing was as it seemed, and she could trust no one—not even Shizuka, despite what the girl had told her. For her family's sake she must steel herself to go through with the marriage to Lord Otori: She had no reason to suspect that the marriage would not go ahead as planned, and yet, she did not believe in it. It seemed as remote as the moon. But if she did not marry—if another man died on her account—there would be no way out for her but her own death.

She tried to face it with courage, but to herself she could not pretend: She was fifteen years old, she did not want to die, she wanted to live and to be with Takeo.

The stifling day was slowly drawing to an end, the watery sun casting an eerie reddish light over the town. Kaede was weary and restless, longing to divest herself of the layers of robes she wore, longing for the coolness and dark of night, yet dreading the next day, and the next.

"The Otori lords came to the castle today, didn't they?" she said, trying to keep the emotion out of her voice.

"Yes, Lord Iida received them." Shizuka hesitated. Kaede felt her eyes on her, and was aware of her pity. Shizuka said quietly, "Lady . . ." She went no further.

"What is it?"

Shizuka began to speak brightly of wedding clothes as two maids passed by outside, their feet making the floor sing. When the sound had died away, Kaede asked, "What were you about to say?"

"You remember I told you that you could kill someone with a needle? I'm going to show you how. You never know, you might need it."

She took out what looked like an ordinary needle, but when Kaede held it she realized it was stronger and heavier, a miniature weapon. Shizuka demonstrated how to drive it into the eye or into the neck.

"Now hide it in the hem of your sleeve. Be careful, don't stick yourself with it."

Kaede shuddered, half-appalled, half-fascinated. "I don't know if I could do it."

"You stabbed a man in rage," Shizuka said.

"You know that?"

"Arai told me. In rage or fear, humans don't know what they are capable of. Keep your knife with you at all times. I wish we had swords, but they are too hard to conceal. The best thing, if it comes to a fight, is to kill a man as soon as possible and take his sword."

"What's going to happen?" Kaede whispered.

"I wish I could tell you everything, but it's too dangerous for you. I just want you to be prepared."

Kaede opened her mouth to question her further, but Shizuka murmured, "You must be silent: Ask me nothing and say nothing to anyone. The less you know, the safer you are."

Kaede had been given a small room at the end of the residence, next to the larger room where the Iida women were, with Lady Maruyama and her daughter. Both rooms opened onto the garden that lay along the southern side of the residence, and she could hear the splash of water and the slight movement of the trees. All night Kaede was aware of Shizuka's wakefulness. Once she sat and saw the girl cross-legged in the doorway, barely visible against the starless sky. Owls hooted in the dark hours, and at dawn from the river came the cries of waterfowl. It began to rain.

She dozed off listening to them, and was woken by the strident calls of crows. The rain had stopped and it was already hot. Shizuka was dressed. When she saw Kaede was awake, she knelt beside her and whispered, "Lady, I have to try to speak to Lord Otori. Will you please get up and write a letter to him, a poem or something? I need a pretext to visit him again."

"What's happened?" Kaede said, alarmed by the girl's drawn face.

"I don't know. Last night I was expecting something. . . . It didn't happen. I have to go and find out why."

In a louder voice she said, "I will prepare ink, but my lady must not be so impatient. You have all day to write suitable poems."

"What shall I write?" Kaede whispered. "I don't know how to write poetry. I never learned."

"It doesn't matter, something about married love, mandarin ducks, the clematis and the wall."

Kaede could almost have believed Shizuka was joking, except that the girl's demeanor was deathly serious.

"Help me dress," she said imperiously. "Yes, I know it is

early, but stop complaining. I must write at once to Lord Otori."

Shizuka smiled encouragingly at her, forcing her mouth in her pale face.

She wrote something, she hardly knew what, and in the loudest voice possible told Shizuka to hurry to the Otori lodging house with it. Shizuka went with a show of reluctance, and Kaede heard her complain quietly to the guards, heard their laughter in response.

She called for the maids to bring her tea and, when she had drunk it, sat gazing out onto the garden, trying to calm her fears, trying to be as courageous as Shizuka. Every now and then her fingers went to the needle in her sleeve, or to the smooth, cool handle of the knife inside her robe. She thought of how Lady Maruyama and Shizuka had taught her to fight. What were they anticipating? She had felt herself a pawn in the game being played around her, but at least they had tried to prepare her, and they had given her weapons.

Shizuka was back within the hour, bringing a letter in return from Lord Otori, a poem written with lightness and skill.

Kaede gazed at it. "What does it mean?"

"It's just an excuse. He had to write something in return."

"Is Lord Otori well?" she asked formally.

"Yes, indeed, and waiting with all his heart for you."

"Tell me the truth," Kaede whispered. She looked at Shizuka's face, saw the hesitation in her eyes. "Lord Takeo—he's dead?"

"We don't know." Shizuka sighed deeply. "I must tell you. He has disappeared with Kenji. Lord Otori believes the Tribe has taken him."

"What does that mean?" She felt the tea she had drunk earlier move in her stomach, and thought for a moment she would vomit.

"Let us walk in the garden while it's still cool," Shizuka said calmly.

Kaede stood and thought she would faint. She felt drops of sweat form, cold and clammy, on her brow. Shizuka held her under the elbow and led her onto the veranda, knelt in front of her, and helped her feet into her sandals.

As they walked slowly down the path among the trees and shrubs, the babble of water from the stream covered their voices. Shizuka whispered quickly and urgently into Kaede's ear.

"Last night there was to be an attempt on Iida's life. Arai is barely thirty miles away with a huge army. The warrior monks at Terayama are poised to take the town of Yamagata. The Tohan could be overthrown."

"What does it have to do with Lord Takeo?"

"He was to be the assassin. He was to climb into the castle last night. But the Tribe took him."

"Takeo? The assassin?" Kaede felt like laughing at such an unlikely idea. Then she remembered the darkness that he retreated to, how he always hid his deftness. She realized she hardly knew what lay beneath the surface, yet she had known that there was something more. She took a deep breath, trying to steady herself.

"Who are the Tribe?"

"Takeo's father was of the Tribe, and he was born with unusual talents."

"Like yours," Kaede said flatly. "And your uncle's."

"Far greater than either of us," Shizuka said. "But you are right: We are also from the Tribe."

"You are a spy? An assassin? Is that why you pretend to be my servant?"

"I don't pretend to be your friend," Shizuka replied

swiftly. "I've told you before that you can trust me. Indeed, Arai himself entrusted you to my care."

"How can I believe that when I have been told so many lies?" Kaede said, and felt the corners of her eyes grow hot.

"I am telling you the truth now," Shizuka said, somber.

Kaede felt the faintness of shock sweep over her and then recede a little, leaving her calm and lucid. "My marriage to Lord Otori—was that arranged to give him a reason to come to Inuyama?"

"Not by him. On his part the marriage was made a condition of Takeo's adoption. But once he had agreed to it, he saw it would give him a reason to bring Takeo into the Tohan stronghold." Shizuka paused and then said very quietly, "Iida and the Otori lords may use the marriage to you as a cover for Shigeru's death. This is partly why I was sent to you: to protect you both."

"My reputation will always be useful," she said bitterly, made all too aware of the power men had over her, and how they used it, regardless. The faintness came over her again.

"You must sit for a while," Shizuka said. The shrubs had given way to a more open garden with a view over the moat and the river to the mountains beyond. A pavilion had been built across the stream, placed to catch every faint trace of breeze. They made their way to it, stepping carefully across the rocks. Cushions had been prepared on the floor, and here they sat down. The flowing water gave a sense of coolness, and kingfishers and swallows swooped through the pavilion with sudden flashes of color. In the pools beyond, lotus flowers lifted their purple-pink blooms, and a few deep-blue irises still flowered at the water's edge, their petals almost the same color as the cushions.

"What does it mean, to be taken by the Tribe?" Kaede asked, her fingers restlessly rubbing the fabric beneath her.

"The family Takeo belongs to, the Kikuta, thought the assassination attempt would fail. They did not want to lose him, so they stepped in to prevent it. My uncle played a role in this."

"And you?"

"No, I was of the opinion that the attempt should be made. I thought Takeo had every chance of succeeding, and no revolt against the Tohan will happen while Iida lives."

I can't believe I'm hearing this, Kaede thought. *I am caught up in such treachery. She speaks of Iida's murder as lightly as if he were a peasant or an outcaste. If anyone heard us, we would be*

125

tortured to death. Despite the growing heat, she shivered.

"What will they do with him?"

"He will become one of them, and his life will become a secret to us and everyone."

So I will never see him again, she thought.

They heard voices coming from the path, and a few moments later Lady Maruyama, her daughter, Mariko, and her companion, Sachie, came across the stream and sat down with them. Lady Maruyama looked as pale as Shizuka had earlier, and her manner was in some indefinable way changed. She had lost some of her rigid self-control. She sent Mariko and Sachie a little way off to play with the shuttlecock toy the girl had brought with her.

Kaede made an effort to converse normally. "Lady Mariko is a lovely girl."

"She has no great beauty, but she is intelligent and kind," her mother replied. "She takes more after her father. Maybe she is lucky. Even beauty is dangerous for a woman. Better not to be desired by men." She smiled bitterly, and then whispered to Shizuka, "We have very little time. I hope I can trust Lady Shirakawa."

"I will say nothing to give you away," Kaede said in a low voice.

"Shizuka, tell me what happened."

"Takeo was taken by the Tribe. That is all Lord Shigeru knows."

"I never thought Kenji would betray him. It must have been a bitter blow."

"He said it was always a desperate gamble. He blames no one. His main concern now is your safety. Yours and the child's."

Kaede's first thought was that Shizuka meant the daughter, Mariko, but she saw the slight flush in Lady Maruyama's face. She pressed her lips together, saying nothing.

"What should we do? Should we try to flee?" Lady Maruyama was twisting the sleeve of her robe with white fingers.

"You must do nothing that would arouse Iida's suspicions."

"Shigeru will not flee?" The lady's voice was reed thin.

"I suggested it, but he says he will not. He is too closely watched, and besides, he feels he can only survive by showing no fear. He must act as though he has perfect trust in the Tohan and the proposed alliance."

"He will go through with the marriage?" Her voice rose.

"He will act as though that is his intention," Shizuka said carefully. "We must also act the same, if we want to save his life."

"Iida has sent messages to me pressing me to accept him," Lady Maruyama said. "I have always refused him for Shigeru's sake." She stared, distraught, into Shizuka's face.

"Lady," Shizuka said, "don't speak of these things. Be patient, be brave. All we can do is wait. We must pretend nothing out of the ordinary has happened, and we must prepare for Lady Kaede's wedding."

"They will use it as a pretext to kill him," Lady Maruyama said. "She is so beautiful and so deadly."

"I don't want to cause any man's death," Kaede cried, "least of all Lord Otori's." Her eyes filled with tears suddenly, and she looked away.

"What a shame you cannot marry Lord Iida and bring death to him!" Lady Maruyama exclaimed.

Kaede flinched as though she had been slapped.

"Forgive me," Lady Maruyama whispered. "I am not myself. I have hardly slept. I am mad with fear—for him, for my daughter, for myself, for our child. You do not deserve my rudeness. You have been caught up in our affairs through no fault of your own. I hope you will not think too badly of me."

She took Kaede's hand and pressed it. "If my daughter and I die, you are my heir. I entrust my land and my people to you. Take care of them well." She looked away, across the river, her eyes bright with tears. "If it is the only way to save his life, he must marry you. But then they will kill him anyway."

At the end of the garden, steps had been cut in the fortification wall down to the moat, where two pleasure boats lay moored. There was a gate across the steps, which Kaede guessed would be closed at nightfall, but which now stood open. The moat and the river could be seen through it. Two guards sat lazily by the wall, looking stupefied by the heat.

"It will be cool today out on the water," Lady Maruyama said. "The boatmen might be bought. . . ."

"I would not advise it, lady," Shizuka said urgently. "If you try to escape, you will arouse Iida's suspicions. Our best chance is to placate him until Arai is closer."

"Arai will not approach Inuyama while Iida lives," Lady Maruyama said. "He will not commit himself to a siege. We have always considered this castle impregnable. It can only fall from within."

She glanced again from the water to the keep. "It traps us," she said. "It holds us in its grip. Yet, I must get away."

"Don't attempt anything rash," Shizuka pleaded.

Mariko came back, complaining it was too hot to play. She was followed by Sachie.

"I will take her inside," Lady Maruyama said. "She has lessons, after all. . . ." Her voice tailed away, and tears sprang in her eyes again. "My poor child," she said. "My poor children." She clasped her hands across her belly.

"Come, lady," Sachie said. "You must lie down."

Kaede felt tears of sympathy in her own eyes. The stones of the keep and the walls around her seemed to press in on her. The crickets' shrill was intense and brain-numbing; the heat seemed to reverberate from the ground. Lady Maruyama was right, she thought: They were all trapped, and there was no way of escaping.

"Do you wish to return to the house?" Shizuka asked her.

"Let's stay here a little longer." It occurred to Kaede that there was one more thing she had to talk about. "Shizuka, you seem able to come and go. The guards trust you."

Shizuka nodded. "I have some of the skills of the Tribe in this respect."

"Out of all of the women here, you are the only one who could escape." Kaede hesitated, not sure how to phrase what she felt she must say. Finally she said abruptly, "If you want to leave, you must go. I do not want you to stay on my account." Then she bit her lip and looked swiftly away, for she did not see how she would survive without the girl she had come to depend on.

"We are safest if none of us tries to leave," Shizuka whispered. "But apart from that, it is out of the question. Unless you order me to go, I will never leave you. Our lives are bound together now." She added, as if to herself, "It is not only men who have honor."

"Lord Arai sent you to me," Kaede said, "and you tell me you are from the Tribe, who asserted their power over Lord Takeo. Are you really free to make such decisions? Do you have the choice of honor?"

"For someone who was taught nothing, Lady Shirakawa knows a great deal," Shizuka said, smiling, and for a moment Kaede felt her heart lighten.

She stayed by the water most of the day, eating only a

131

little. The ladies of the household came to join her for a few hours, and they spoke of the beauty of the garden and the wedding arrangements. One of them had been to Hagi, and she described the city with admiration, telling Kaede some of the legends of the Otori clan, whispering of their ancient feud with the Tohan. They all expressed their joy that Kaede was to put an end to this feud, and told her how delighted Lord Iida was with the alliance.

Not knowing how to reply, and aware of the treachery beneath the wedding plans, Kaede sought refuge in shyness, smiled until her face ached, but hardly spoke.

She glanced away and saw Lord Iida in person crossing the garden, in the direction of the pavilion, accompanied by three or four of his retainers.

The ladies immediately fell silent. Kaede called to Shizuka, "I think I will go inside. My head aches."

"I will comb out your hair and massage your head," Shizuka said, and indeed the weight of her hair seemed intolerable to Kaede. Her body felt sticky and chafed beneath the robes. She longed for coolness, for night.

However, as they moved away from the pavilion, Lord

Abe left the group of men and strode towards them. Shizuka immediately dropped to her knees, and Kaede bowed to him, though not as deeply.

"Lady Shirakawa," he said, "Lord Iida wishes to speak to you."

Trying to hide her reluctance, she returned to the pavilion, where Iida was already seated on the cushions. The women had withdrawn and were engaged in looking at the river.

Kaede knelt on the wooden floor, lowering her head to the ground, aware of his deep eyes, pools of molten iron, sweeping over her.

"You may sit up," he said briefly. His voice was rough and the polite forms sat uneasily on his tongue. She felt the gaze of his men, the heavy silence that had become familiar to her, the mixture of lust and admiration.

"Shigeru is a lucky man," Iida said, and she heard both threat and malice in the men's laughter. She thought he would speak to her about the wedding or about her father, who had already sent messages to say he could not attend, due to his wife's illness. His next words surprised her.

"I believe Arai is an old acquaintance of yours?"

"I knew him when he served Lord Noguchi," she replied carefully.

"It was on your account that Noguchi exiled him," Iida said. "Noguchi made a grave mistake, and he's paid for it severely. Now it seems I'm going to have to deal with Arai on my own doorstep." He sighed deeply. "Your marriage to Lord Otori comes at a very good time."

Kaede thought, *I am an ignorant girl, brought up by the Noguchi, loyal and stupid. I know nothing of the intrigues of the clans.*

She made her face doll-like, her voice childish. "I only want to do what Lord Iida and my father want for me."

"You heard nothing on your journey of Arai's movements? Shigeru did not discuss them at any time?"

"I have heard nothing from Lord Arai since he left Lord Noguchi," she replied.

"Yet, they say he was quite a champion of yours."

She dared to look up at him through her eyelashes. "I cannot be held responsible for the way men feel about me, lord."

Their eyes met for a moment. His look was penetrating, predatory. She felt he also desired her, like all the others, piqued and tantalized by the idea that involvement with her brought death.

Revulsion rose in her throat. She thought of the needle concealed in her sleeve, imagined sliding it into his flesh.

"No," he agreed, "nor can we blame any man for admiring you." He spoke over his shoulder to Abe: "You were right. She is exquisite." It was as if he spoke of an inanimate piece of art. "You were going inside? Don't let me detain you. I believe your health is delicate."

"Lord Iida." She bowed to the ground again and shuffled backwards to the edge of the pavilion. Shizuka helped her to her feet and they walked away.

Neither of them spoke until they were back in the room. Then Kaede whispered, "He knows everything."

"No," Shizuka said, taking up the comb and beginning to work on Kaede's hair. "He is not sure. He has no proof of anything. You did well." Her fingers massaged Kaede's scalp and temples. Some of the tension began to ease.

Kaede leaned back against her. "I would like to go to Hagi. Will you come with me?"

"If that comes to pass, you won't need me," Shizuka replied, smiling.

"I think I will always need you," Kaede said. A wistful note crept into her voice. "Maybe I would be happy with Lord Shigeru. If I hadn't met Takeo, if he did not love—"

"Shush, shush." Shizuka sighed, her fingers working and stroking.

"We might have had children," Kaede went on, her voice dreamy and slow. "None of that is going to happen now, yet I must pretend it will."

"We are on the brink of war," Shizuka whispered. "We do not know what will happen in the next few days, let alone the future."

"Where would Lord Takeo be now? Do you know?"

"If he is still in the capital, in one of the secret houses of the Tribe. But they may have already moved him out of the fief."

"Will I ever see him again?" Kaede said, but she didn't expect an answer, nor did Shizuka give one. Her fingers worked on. Beyond the open doors, the garden shimmered in the heat, the crickets more strident than ever.

Slowly the day faded and the shadows began to lengthen.

· 5 ·

I was unconscious for a few moments only. When I came round I was in the dark, and guessed at once I was inside the cart. There were at least two people inside with me. One, I could tell from his breathing, was Kenji, the other, from her perfume, one of the girls. They were pinioning me, one arm each.

I felt terribly sick, as though I'd been hit on the head. The movement of the cart didn't help.

"I'm going to vomit," I said, and Kenji let go of one arm. The sickness half-rose in my throat as I sat up. I realized the girl had let go of my other arm. I forgot about vomiting in my desperate desire to escape. I threw myself, arms across my head, at the hinged opening of the cart.

It was firmly fastened from the outside. I felt the skin on one hand tear against a nail. Kenji and the girl grabbed me, forcing me down as I struggled and thrashed. Someone outside called out, a sharp angry warning.

Kenji swore at me. "Shut up! Lie still! If the Tohan find you now, you're dead!"

But I had gone beyond reason. When I was a boy I used to bring wild animals home, fox cubs, stoats, baby rabbits. I could never tame them. All they wanted, blindly, irrationally, was to escape. I thought of that blind rush now. Nothing mattered to me except that Shigeru should not believe I had betrayed him. I would never stay with the Tribe. They would never be able to keep me.

"Shut him up," Kenji whispered to the girl as he struggled to hold me still, and under her hands the world went sickening and black again.

The next time I came around I truly believed I was dead and in the underworld. I could not see or hear. It was pitch-dark and everything had gone completely silent. Then feeling began to return. I hurt too much all over to be dead. My throat was raw, one hand throbbed, the other wrist ached where it had been bent backwards. I tried to sit up, but I was tied up in some way, loosely with soft bindings, just enough to restrain me. I turned my head, shaking it. There was a blindfold across my eyes, but it was being deafened that seemed the worst thing. After a few moments I realized that my ears had been plugged with something. I felt a surge of relief that I had not lost my hearing.

A hand against my face made me jump. The blindfold was removed and I saw Kenji kneeling beside me. An oil lamp burned on the floor next to him, lighting his face. I thought fleetingly how dangerous he was. Once he had sworn to protect me with his life. The last thing I wanted now was his protection.

His mouth moved as he spoke.

"I can't hear anything," I said. "Take the plugs out."

He did so, and my world returned to me. I stayed without speaking for a few moments, placing myself in it again. I could hear the river in the distance: So I was still in Inuyama. The house I was in was silent, everyone sleeping except guards. I could hear them whispering inside the gate. I guessed it was late at night, and at that moment heard the midnight bell from a distant temple.

I should have been inside the castle now.

"I'm sorry we hurt you," Kenji said. "You didn't need to struggle so much."

I could feel the bitter rage about to erupt inside me again. I tried to control it. "Where am I?"

"In one of the Tribe houses. We'll move you out of the capital in a day or two."

His calm, matter-of-fact voice infuriated me further. "You said you would never betray him, the night of my adoption. Do you remember?"

Kenji sighed. "We both spoke that night of conflicting obligations. Shigeru knows I serve the Tribe first. I warned him then, and often since, that the Tribe has a prior claim to you, and that sooner or later it would make it."

"Why now?" I said bitterly. "You could have left me for one more night."

"Maybe I personally would have given you that chance. But the incident at Yamagata pushed things beyond my control. Anyway, you would be dead by now, and no use to anyone."

"I could have killed Iida first," I muttered.

"That outcome was considered," Kenji said, "and judged not to be in the best interests of the Tribe."

"I suppose most of you work for him?"

"We work for whoever pays us best. We like a stable society. Open warfare makes it hard to operate. Iida's rule is harsh but stable. It suits us."

"You were deceiving Shigeru all the time, then?"

"As no doubt he has often deceived me." Kenji was silent for a good minute, and then went on, "Shigeru was doomed from the start. Too many powerful people want to get rid of him. He has played well to survive this far."

A chill came over me. "He must not die," I whispered.

"Iida will certainly seize on some pretext to kill him," Kenji said mildly. "He has become far too dangerous to be allowed to live. Quite apart from the fact that he offended Iida personally—the affair with Lady Maruyama, your adoption—the scenes at Yamagata alarmed the Tohan profoundly." The lamp flickered and smoked. Kenji added quietly, "The problem with Shigeru is, people love him."

"We can't abandon him! Let me go back to him."

"It's not my decision," Kenji replied. "Even if it were, I

could not do it now. Iida knows you are from the Hidden. He would hand you over to Ando as he promised. Shigeru, no doubt, will have a warrior's death, swift, honorable. You would be tortured: You know what they do."

I was silent. My head ached, and an unbearable sense of failure was creeping over me. Everything in me had been aimed like a spear at one target. Now the hand that had held me had been removed and I had fallen, useless, to the earth.

"Give up, Takeo," Kenji said, watching my face. "It's over."

I nodded slowly. I might as well pretend to agree. "I'm terribly thirsty."

"I'll make some tea. It will help you sleep. Do you want anything to eat?"

"No. Can you untie me?"

"Not tonight," Kenji replied.

I thought about that while I was drifting in and out of sleep, trying to find a comfortable position to lie in with my hands and feet tied. I decided it meant Kenji thought I could escape, once I was untied, and if my teacher thought I could, then it was probably true. It was the only comforting thought I had, and it did not console me for long.

Towards dawn it began raining. I listened to the gutters filling, the eaves dripping. Then the cocks began to crow and the town woke. I heard the servants stirring in the house, smelled smoke as fires were lit in the kitchen. I listened to the voices and the footsteps, and counted them, mapping the layout of the house, where it stood in the street, what was on either side. From the smells and the sounds as work began I guessed I was hidden within a brewery, one of the big merchant houses on the edge of the castle town. The room I was in had no exterior windows. It was as narrow as an eel's bed and remained dark even long after sunrise.

The wedding was to be held the day after tomorrow. Would Shigeru survive till then? And if he was murdered before, what would happen to Kaede? My thoughts tormented me. How would Shigeru spend these next two days? What was he doing now? What was he thinking of me? The idea that he might imagine I had run away of my own free will was agony to me. And what would be the opinion of the Otori men? They would despise me.

I called to Kenji that I needed to use the privy. He untied my feet and took me there. We stepped out of the small room into a larger one, and then downstairs into the rear courtyard. A maid came with a bowl of water and helped me wash my hands. There was a lot of blood on me, more than seemed likely from the one cut from the nail. I must have done some damage with my knife to someone. I wondered where the knife was now.

When we went back into the secret room Kenji left my feet untied.

"What happens next?" I asked.

"Try and sleep longer. Nothing will happen today."

"Sleep! I feel as if I will never sleep again!"

Kenji studied me for a moment and then said briefly, "It will all pass."

If my hands had been free, I would have killed him. I leaped at him as I was, swinging my bound hands to catch him in the side. I took him by surprise, and we both went flying, but he turned beneath me as quick as a snake and pinioned me to the ground. If I was enraged, so now was he. I'd seen him exasperated with me before, but now he was furious. He struck me twice across the face, real blows that shook my teeth and left me dizzy.

"Give up!" he shouted. "I'll beat you into it if I have to. Is that what you want?"

"Yes!" I shouted back. "Go ahead and kill me. It's the only way you'll keep me here!"

I arched my back and rolled sideways, getting rid of his weight, trying to kick and bite. He struck me again, but I got away from him and, swearing at him in rage, flung myself against him.

I heard rapid steps outside, and the doors slid open. The girl from Yamagata and one of the young men ran into the room. The three of them subdued me eventually, but I was more than half-mad with fury, and it took a while before they could tie my feet again.

Kenji was seething with anger. The girl and the young man looked from me to him and back again. "Master," the girl said, "leave him with us. We'll watch him for a while. You need some rest." Clearly they were astonished and shocked by his loss of control.

We had been together for months as master and pupil. He had taught me almost everything I knew. I had obeyed him without question, had put up with his nagging, his sarcasm, and his chastisements. I had put aside my initial suspicions and had come to trust him. All that was shattered as far as I was concerned, and would never be restored.

Now he knelt in front of me, seized my head, and forced me to look at him. "I'm trying to save your life!" he shouted. "Can't you get that into your thick skull?"

I spat at him and braced myself for another blow, but the young man restrained him.

"Go, master," he urged him.

Kenji let go of me and stood up. "What stubborn, crazy blood did you get from your mother?" he demanded. When he reached the door he turned and said, "Watch him all the time. Don't untie him."

When he had gone I wanted to scream and sob like a child in a tantrum. Tears of rage and despair pricked my eyelids. I lay back on the mattress, face turned towards the wall.

The girl left the room shortly after and came back with cold water and a cloth. She made me sit up and wiped my face. My lip was split, and I could feel the bruising around one eye and across the cheekbone. Her gentleness made me feel she had a certain sympathy towards me, though she said nothing.

The young man watched without speaking, either.

Later she brought tea and some food. I drank the tea but refused to eat anything.

"Where's my knife?" I said.

"We have it," she replied.

"Did I cut you?"

"No, that was Keiko. Both she and Akio were wounded on the hand, but not too badly."

"I wish I had killed you all."

"I know," she replied. "No one can say that you didn't fight. But you had five members of the Tribe against you. There is no shame."

Shame, however, was what I felt seeping through me as though it stained my white bones black.

The long day passed, oppressive and slow. The evening bell had just rung from the temple at the end of the street when Keiko came to the door and spoke in a whisper to my two guards. I could hear what she said perfectly well, though out of habit I pretended not to. Someone had come to see me, someone called Kikuta.

A few minutes later a lean man of medium height stepped into the room, followed by Kenji. There was a similarity between them, the same shifting look that made them unremarkable. This man's skin was darker, closer to my own in color. His hair was still black, although he must have been nearly forty years old.

He stood and looked at me for a few moments, then crossed the room, knelt beside me, and, as Kenji had the first time he met me, took my hands and turned them palms up.

"Why is he tied up?" he said. His voice was unremarkable, too, though the intonation was northern.

"He tries to escape, master," the girl said. "He is calmer now, but he has been very wild."

"Why do you want to escape?" he asked me. "You are finally where you belong."

"I don't belong here," I replied. "Before I had even heard of the Tribe, I swore allegiance to Lord Otori. I am legally adopted into the Otori clan."

"Unnh," he grunted. "The Otori call you Takeo, I hear. What is your real name?"

I did not reply.

"He was raised among the Hidden," Kenji said quietly. "The name he was given at birth was Tomasu."

Kikuta hissed through his teeth. "That's best forgotten," he said. "Takeo will do for the time being, though it's never been a Tribe name. Do you know who I am?"

"No," I said, though I had a very good idea.

"No, master." The young guard couldn't help the whispered reproof.

Kikuta smiled. "Did you not teach him manners, Kenji?"

"Courtesy is for those who deserve it," I said.

"You will learn that I do deserve it. I am the head of your family, Kikuta Kotaro, first cousin to your father."

"I never knew my father, and I have never used his name."

"But you are stamped with Kikuta traits: the sharpness of hearing, artistic ability, all the other talents we know you have in abundance, as well as the line on your palms. These are things you can't deny."

From away in the distance came a faint sound, a tap at the front door of the shop below. I heard someone slide the door open and speak, an unimportant conversation about wine. Kikuta's head had also turned slightly. I felt something: the beginnings of recognition.

"Do you hear everything?" I said.

"Not as much as you. It fades with age. But pretty well everything."

"At Terayama, the young man there, the monk, said, 'Like a dog.'" A bitter note crept into my voice. "'Useful to your masters,' he said. Is that why you kidnapped me, because I will be useful to you?"

"It's not a question of being useful," he said. "It's a matter of being born into the Tribe. This is where you belong. You would still belong if you had no talents at all, and if you had all the talents in the world, but were not born into the Tribe, you could never belong and we would have no interest in you. As it is, your father was Kikuta: You are Kikuta."

"I have no choice?"

He smiled again. "It's not something you choose, any more than you chose to have sharp hearing."

This man was calming me in some way as I had calmed horses: by understanding my nature. I had never met anyone before who knew what it was like to be Kikuta. I could feel it exerting an attraction on me.

"Suppose I accept that; what will you do with me?"

"Find you somewhere safe, in another province, away from the Tohan, while you finish your training."

"I don't want any more training. I am done with teachers!"

"Muto Kenji was sent to Hagi because of his long-standing friendship with Shigeru. He has taught you a lot, but Kikuta should be taught by Kikuta."

I was no longer listening. "Friendship? He deceived and betrayed him!"

Kikuta's voice went quiet. "You have great skills, Takeo, and no one's doubting your courage or your heart. It's just your head that needs sorting out. You have to learn to control your emotions."

"So I can betray old friends as easily as Muto Kenji?" The brief moment of calm had passed. I could feel the rage about to erupt again. I wanted to surrender to it, because it was only rage that wiped out shame. The two young people stepped forward, ready to restrain me, but Kikuta waved them back. He himself took my bound hands and held them firmly.

"Look at me," he said.

Despite myself, my eyes met his. I could feel myself drowning in the whirlpool of my emotions, and only his eyes kept me from going under. Slowly the rage abated. A tremendous weariness took its place. I could not fight the sleep that rolled towards me like clouds over the mountain. Kikuta's eyes held me until my own eyes closed, and the mist swallowed me up.

When I woke, it was daylight, the sun slanting into the room beyond the secret one and throwing a dim orange light into where I lay. I couldn't believe it was afternoon again: I must have slept for nearly a whole day. The girl was sitting on the floor a little way from me. I realized the door had just closed; the sound had wakened me. The other guard must have just stepped out.

"What's your name?" I said. My voice was croaky, my throat still sore.

"Yuki."

"And him?"

"Akio."

He was the one she'd said I'd wounded. "What did that man do to me?"

"The Kikuta master? He just put you to sleep. It's something Kikuta can do."

I remembered the dogs in Hagi. Something Kikuta can do . . .

"What hour is it?" I said.

"First half of the Rooster."

"Is there any news?"

"Of Lord Otori? Nothing." She came a little closer and whispered, "Do you want me to take a message to him?"

I stared at her. "Can you?"

"I've worked as a maid at the place he is lodged in, as I did at Yamagata." She gave me a look full of meaning. "I can try and speak to him tonight or tomorrow morning."

"Tell him I did not leave voluntarily. Ask him to forgive me. . . ." There was far too much to try to put into words. I broke off. "Why would you do this for me?"

She shook her head, smiled, and indicated we should say no more. Akio returned to the room. One of his hands was bandaged, and he treated me coldly.

Later they untied my feet and took me to the bath, undressed me, and helped me into the hot water. I was moving like a cripple and every muscle in my body ached.

"It's what you do to yourself when you go mad with rage," Yuki said. "You have no idea how much you can hurt yourself with your own strength."

"That's why you have to learn self-control," Akio added. "Otherwise you are only a danger to others as well as yourself."

When they took me back to the room he said, "You broke every rule of the Tribe with your disobedience. Let this be a punishment to you."

I realized it was not only resentment for my wounding him: He disliked me and was jealous too. I didn't care one way or the other. My head ached fiercely, and although the rage had left me, it had been replaced with the deepest sorrow.

My guards seemed to accept that some sort of truce had been reached, and left me untied. I was in no condition to go anywhere. I could hardly walk, let alone climb out of windows and scale roofs. I ate a little, the first food I had taken in two days. Yuki and Akio left, their places taken by Keiko and the other young man, whose name was Yoshinori. Keiko's hands were also bandaged. They both seemed as hostile towards me as Akio. We did not talk at all.

I thought of Shigeru and prayed that Yuki would be able to speak to him. Then I found myself praying in the manner of the Hidden, the words coming unbidden onto my tongue. I had absorbed them, after all, with my mother's milk. Like a child I whispered them to myself, and maybe they brought me comfort, for after a while I slept again, deeply.

The sleep refreshed me. When I woke, it was morning; my body had recovered a little and I could move without pain. Yuki was back, and when she saw I was awake, she dispatched Akio on some errand. She seemed older than the others, and had some authority over them.

She told me immediately what I longed to hear. "I went to the lodging house last night and managed to speak to Lord Otori. He was greatly relieved to hear you are unharmed. His main fear was that you had been captured or murdered by the Tohan. He wrote to you yesterday, in the vain hope you might be able to retrieve the letter someday."

"You have it?"

She nodded. "He gave me something else for you. I hid it in the closet."

She slid open the door to the closet where the bedding was stored, and from beneath a pile of quilts took out a long bundle. I recognized the cloth: It was an old traveling robe of Shigeru's, maybe the very one he had been wearing when he had saved my life in Mino. She put it in my hands and I held it up to my face. There was something rigid wrapped up inside it. I knew immediately what it was. I unfolded the robe and lifted Jato out.

I thought I would die of grief. Tears fell then: I could not prevent them.

Yuki said gently, "They are to go unarmed to the castle for the wedding. He did not want the sword to be lost if he did not return."

"He will not return," I said, the tears streaming like a river.

Yuki took the sword from me and rewrapped it, stowing it away again in the closet.

"Why did you do this for me?" I said. "Surely you are disobeying the Tribe?"

"I am from Yamagata," she replied. "I was there when Takeshi was murdered. The family who died with him—I grew up with their daughter. You saw what it was like in Yamagata, how much the people love Shigeru. I am one of them. And I believe Kenji, the Muto master, has wronged both of you." There was a note of challenge in her voice that sounded almost like an outraged—and disobedient—child. I did not want to question her further. I was just immensely grateful for what she had done for me.

"Give me the letter," I said after a while.

He had been taught by Ichiro and his handwriting was everything mine should have been but wasn't, bold and flowing: *Takeo, I am most happy that you are safe. There is nothing to forgive. I know that you would not betray me, and I always knew that the Tribe would try to take you. Think of me tomorrow.*

The main letter followed. . . .

Takeo, for whatever reasons, we could not follow through with our gamble. I have many regrets, but am spared the sorrow of sending you to your death. I believe you to be with the Tribe; your destiny is therefore out of my hands. However, you are my adopted son and my only legal heir. I hope one day you will be able to take up your Otori inheritance. If I die at Iida's hands, I charge you to avenge my death, but not to mourn it, for I believe I will achieve more in death than in life. Be patient. I also ask that you will look after Lady Shirakawa.

Some bond from a former life must have decreed the strength of our feelings. I am glad we met at Mino. I embrace you.

Your adopted father, Shigeru.

It was set with his seal.

"The Otori men believe you and the Muto master to have been murdered," Yuki said. "No one believes you would have left voluntarily. I thought you would like to know."

I thought of them all, the men who had teased and spoiled me, taught me and put up with me, been proud of me, and still thought the best of me. They were going to certain death, but I envied them, for they would die with Shigeru, while I was condemned to live, starting with that terrible day.

Every sound from outside made me start. At one time, soon after midday, I thought I heard far in the distance the clash of swords and the screams of men, but no one came to tell me anything. An oppressive and unnatural silence settled over the town.

My only consolation was the thought of Jato, lying hidden within arm's reach. Many times I was on the point of seizing the sword and fighting my way out of the house, but Shigeru's last message to me had been to be patient. Rage had given way to grief, but now, as my tears dried, grief gave way to determination. I would not throw away my life unless I took Iida with me.

Around the hour of the Monkey I heard a voice in the shop below. My heart stopped, for I knew it was news of some sort. Keiko and Yoshinori were with me, but after about ten minutes Yuki came and told them they were to go.

She knelt beside me and put her hand on my arm. "Muto Shizuka has sent a message from the castle. The masters are coming to speak to you."

"Is he dead?"

"No, worse: He is captured. They will tell you."

"He is to kill himself?"

Yuki hesitated. She spoke swiftly without looking at me. "Iida has accused him of harboring a member of the Hidden—of being one of them himself. Ando has a personal feud against him and is demanding punishment. Lord Otori has been stripped of the privileges of the warrior class and is to be treated as a common criminal."

"Iida would not dare," I said.

"He has already done it."

I heard footsteps approaching from the outer room as outrage and shock sent energy flooding through me. I leaped at the closet and pulled out the sword, drawing it in the same movement from the sheath. I felt it cleave to my hands. I raised it above my head.

Kenji and Kikuta stepped into the room. They went very still when they saw Jato in my hands. Kikuta reached inside his robe for a knife, but Kenji did not move.

"I am not going to attack you," I said, "though you deserve to die. But I will kill myself. . . ."

Kenji rolled his eyes upwards. Kikuta said mildly, "We

hope you won't have to resort to that." Then after a moment he hissed and went on almost impatiently, "Sit down, Takeo. You've made your point."

We all lowered ourselves onto the floor. I placed the sword on the matting next to me.

"I see Jato found you," Kenji said. "I should have expected that."

"I brought it, master," Yuki said.

"No, the sword used you. So it goes from hand to hand. I should know: It used me to find Shigeru after Yaegahara."

"Where is Shizuka?" I said.

"Still in the castle. She did not come herself. Just to send a message was very dangerous, but she wanted us to know what happened, and asked what we intended to do about it."

"Tell me."

"Lady Maruyama tried to flee from the castle yesterday with her daughter." Kikuta's voice was level and dispassionate. "She bribed some boatmen to take her across the river. They were betrayed and intercepted. All three women threw themselves into the water. The lady and her daughter drowned, but the servant, Sachie, was rescued. Better for her that she had drowned, for she was then tortured until she revealed the relationship with Shigeru, the alliance with Arai, and the lady's connection with the Hidden."

"The pretense that the wedding would take place was maintained until Shigeru was inside the castle," Kenji said. "Then the Otori men were cut down, and he was accused of treason." He paused for a moment and then continued quietly, "He is already strung from the castle wall."

"Crucified?" I whispered.

"Hung by the arms."

I closed my eyes briefly, imagining the pain, the dislocation of the shoulders, the slow suffocation, the terrible humiliation.

"'A warrior's death, swift and honorable'?" I said, in accusation, to Kenji.

He did not reply. His face, usually so mobile, was still, his pale skin, white.

I put my hand out and touched Jato. I said to Kikuta, "I have a proposition to put to the Tribe. I believe you work for whoever pays you most. I will buy my services from you with something you seem to value—that is, my life and my obedience. Let me go tonight and bring him down. In return I will give up the name of Otori and join the Tribe. If you don't agree, I will end my life here. I will never leave this room."

The two masters exchanged a glance. Kenji nodded imperceptibly. Kikuta said, "I have to accept that the situation has changed, and we seem to have come to a stalemate." There was a sudden flurry in the street, feet running and shouts. We both listened in an identical Kikuta way. The sounds faded, and he went on, "I accept your proposal. You have my permission to go into the castle tonight."

"I will go with him," Yuki said, "and I'll prepare everything we may need."

"If the Muto master agrees."

"I agree," Kenji said. "I will come too."

"You don't need to," I said.

"All the same, I'm coming with you."

"Do we know where Arai is?" I asked.

Kenji said, "Even if he were to march all night, he would not be here before daybreak."

"But he is on his way?"

"Shizuka believes he will not move against the castle. His only hope is to provoke Iida into fighting him on the border."

"And Terayama?"

"They will erupt when they hear of this outrage," Yuki said. "The town of Yamagata too."

"No revolt will succeed while Iida lives, and anyway, these wider concerns are not ours," Kikuta interrupted with a flash of anger. "You may bring Shigeru's body down; our agreement covers nothing more."

I said nothing. *While Iida lives . . .*

It was raining again, the gentle sound enveloping the town, washing tiles and cobbles, freshening the stale air.

"What of Lady Shirakawa?" I said.

"Shizuka says she is in shock, but calm. No suspicion seems to be attached to her, apart from the blame that goes with her unfortunate reputation. People say she is cursed, but she is not suspected of being part of the conspiracy. Sachie, the servant, was weaker than the Tohan thought, and she escaped their torture into death before, it seems, incriminating Shizuka."

"Did she reveal anything about me?"

Kenji sighed, "She knew nothing, except that you were from the Hidden and rescued by Shigeru, which Iida knew already. He and Ando think Shigeru adopted you purely to insult them, and that you fled when you were recognized. They do not suspect your Tribe identity, and they do not know of your skills."

That was one advantage. Another was the weather and the night. The rain lessened to a drizzling mist; the cloud cover was dense and low, completely obscuring moon and stars. And the third was the change that had come over me. Something inside me that had been half-formed before had set into its intended shape. My outburst of mad rage, followed by the profound Kikuta sleep, had burned away the dross from my nature and left a core of steel. I recognized in myself the glimpses I'd had of Kenji's true self, as if Jato had come to life.

The three of us went through the equipment and clothing. After that I spent an hour exercising. My muscles were still stiff, though less sore. My right wrist bothered me the most. When I'd raised Jato before, the pain had shot back to the elbow. In the end Yuki strapped it up for me with a leather wrist guard.

Towards the second half of the hour of the Dog, we ate lightly and then sat in silence, slowing breathing and heartbeat. We darkened the room to improve our night vision. An early curfew had been imposed, and after the horsemen had patrolled the streets, driving people inside, the streets were quiet. Around us the house sang its evening song: dishes being cleared away, dogs fed, guards settling down for the night watch. I could hear the tread of maids as they went to spread out the bedding, the click of the abacus from the front room as someone did the day's accounts. Gradually the song dwindled to a few constant notes: the deep breathing of the sleeping, occasional snores, once the cry of a man at the moment of physical passion. These mundane human sounds touched my soul. I found myself thinking of my father, of his longing to live an ordinary human life. Had he cried out like that when I was conceived?

After a while Kenji told Yuki to leave us alone for a few minutes and came to sit beside me. He said in a low voice, "The accusation of being connected with the Hidden—how far does that go?"

"He never mentioned it to me, other than to change my name from Tomasu and warn me against praying."

"The rumor is that he would not deny it; he refused to defile the images." Kenji's voice was puzzled, almost irritated.

"The first time I met Lady Maruyama, she traced the

sign of the Hidden on my hand," I said slowly.

"He kept so much concealed from me," Kenji said. "I thought I knew him!"

"Did he know of the lady's death?"

"Apparently Iida told him with delight."

I thought about this for a few moments. I knew Shigeru would have refused to deny the beliefs Lady Maruyama held so deeply. Whether he believed them or not, he would never submit to Iida's bullying. And now he was keeping the promise he had made to her in Chigawa. He would marry no other woman and he would not live without her.

"I couldn't know Iida would treat him like this," Kenji said. I felt he was trying to excuse himself in some way, but the betrayal was too great for me to forgive. I was glad he was coming with me, and thankful for his skills, but after this night I never wanted to see him again.

"Let's go and bring him down," I said. I got up and called quietly to Yuki. She came back into the room and the three of us put on the dark night attire of the Tribe, covering our faces and hands so no inch of skin showed. We took garrotes, ropes and grapples, long and short knives, and poison capsules that would give us a swift death.

I took up Jato. Kenji said, "Leave it here. You can't climb with a long sword." I ignored him. I knew what I would need it for.

The house I'd been hidden in was well to the west of the castle town, among the merchants' houses south of the river. The area was crisscrossed with many narrow alleys and laneways, making it easy to move through unseen. At the end of the street we passed the temple, where lights still burned as the priests prepared for the midnight rituals. A cat sat beside a stone lantern. It did not stir as we slipped by.

We were approaching the river when I heard the chink of steel and the tramp of feet. Kenji went invisible in a gateway. Yuki and I leaped silently onto the roof of the wall and merged into the tiles.

The patrol consisted of a man on horseback and six foot soldiers. Two of them carried flaming torches. They progressed along the road that ran beside the river, lighting each alleyway and peering down it. They made a great deal of noise, and so did not alarm me at all.

The tiles against my face were damp and slippery. The mild drizzle continued, muffling sound.

The rain would be falling on Shigeru's face. . . .

I dropped from the wall, and we went on towards the river.

A small canal ran alongside the alley. Yuki led us into it where it disappeared into a drain beneath the road. We crawled through it, disturbing the sleeping fish, and emerged where it flowed into the river, the water masking our foot-steps. The dark bulk of the castle loomed in front of us. The cloud cover was so low that I could barely make out the highest towers. Between us and the fortification wall lay first the river, then the moat.

"Where is he?" I whispered to Kenji.

"On the east side, below Iida's palace. Where we saw the iron rings."

Bile rose in my throat. Fighting it back, I said, "Guards?"

"In the corridor immediately above, stationary. On the ground below, patrols."

As I had done at Yamagata, I sat and looked at the castle for a long time. None of us spoke. I could feel the dark Kikuta self rising, flowing into vein and muscle. So would I flow into the castle, and force it to give up what it held.

I took Jato from my belt and laid it on the bank, hiding it in the long grass. "Wait there," I said silently. "I will bring your master to you."

We slipped one by one into the river and swam beneath the surface to the far bank. I could hear the first patrol in the gardens beyond the moat. We lay in the reeds until it had passed, then ran over the narrow strip of marshland and swam in the same way across the moat.

The first fortification wall rose straight from the moat. At the top was a small tiled wall that ran all the way round the garden in front of the residence and the narrow strip of land behind, between the residence walls and the fortification wall. Kenji dropped onto the ground to watch for patrols while Yuki and I crept along the tiled roof to the southeast corner. Twice we heard Kenji's warning cricket's chirp and went invisible on top of the wall while the patrols passed below us.

I knelt and looked upwards. Above me was the row of windows of the corridor at the back of the residence. They were all closed and barred, save one, closest to the iron rings from which Shigeru was suspended, a rope around each wrist. His head hung forward on his chest, and I thought he was already dead, but then I saw that his feet were braced slightly against the wall, taking some of the weight from his arms. I could hear the slow rasp of his breath. He was still alive.

The nightingale floor sang. I flattened myself back onto the tiles. I heard someone lean from the window above, and then a cry of pain from Shigeru as the rope was jerked and his feet slipped.

"Dance, Shigeru, it's your wedding day!" the guard jeered.

I could feel the slow burn of rage. Yuki laid one hand on my arm, but I was not going to erupt. My rage was cold now, and all the more powerful.

We waited there for a long time. No more patrols passed below. Had Kenji silenced them all? The lamp in the window flickered and smoked. Someone came there every ten minutes or so. Each time the suffering man at the end of the ropes found a foothold, one of the guards came and shook him loose. Each time the cry of pain was weaker, and it took him longer to recover.

The window remained open. I whispered to Yuki. "We must climb up. If you can kill them as they come back, I'll take the rope. Cut the wrist ropes when you hear the deer bark. I'll lower him down."

"I'll meet you at the canal," she mouthed.

Immediately after the next visit from the torturers, we dropped to the ground, crossed the narrow strip of land, and began to scale the residence wall. Yuki climbed in through the window while I, clinging to the ledge beneath it, took the rope from my waist and lashed it to one of the iron rings.

The nightingales sang. Invisible, I froze against the wall. I heard someone lean out above me, heard the slightest gasp, the thud of feet kicking helplessly against the garrote, then silence.

Yuki whispered, "Go!"

I began to climb down the wall towards Shigeru, the rope paying out as I went. I had nearly reached him when I heard the cricket chirp. Again I went invisible, praying the mist would hide the extra rope. I heard the patrol pass below me. There was a sound from the moat, a sudden splash. Their attention was distracted by it. One of the men went towards the edge of the wall, holding his torch out over the water. The light shone dully off a white wall of mist.

"Just a water rat," he called. The men disappeared and I heard their footsteps fade slowly away.

Now time speeded up. I knew another guard would soon appear above me. How much longer could Yuki kill them off one by one? The walls were slippery, the rope even more so. I slithered down the last few feet until I was level with Shigeru.

His eyes were closed, but he either heard or felt my

171

presence. He opened them, whispered my name without surprise, and gave the ghost of his openhearted smile, breaking my heart again.

I said, "This will hurt. Don't make a sound."

He closed his eyes again and braced his feet against the wall.

I tied him to me as firmly as I could and barked like a deer to Yuki. She slashed the ropes that held Shigeru. He gasped despite himself as his arms were freed. The extra weight dislodged me from the slippery surface of the wall, and we both fell towards the ground as I prayed that my rope would hold. It brought us up short but with a terrible jolt, with about four feet to spare.

Kenji stepped out of the darkness and together we untied Shigeru and carried him to the wall.

Kenji threw the grapples up and we managed to drag him over. Then we tied the rope to him again and Kenji lowered him down the wall while I climbed down alongside, trying to ease him a little.

We could not stop at the bottom, but had to swim him straightaway across the moat, covering his face with a black hood. Without the mist we would have been immediately discovered, for we could not take him underwater. Then we carried him across the last strip of castle land to the riverbank. By this time he was barely conscious, sweating from pain, his lips raw where he had bitten them to prevent himself from crying out. Both shoulders were dislocated, as I had expected, and he was coughing up blood from some internal injury.

It was raining more heavily. A real deer barked as we startled it, and it bounded away, but there was no sound from the castle. We took Shigeru into the river and swam gently and slowly to the opposite bank. I was blessing the rain, for it masked us, muffling every sound, but it also meant that when I looked back at the castle, I could see no sign of Yuki.

When we reached the bank we laid him down in the long summer grass. Kenji knelt beside him and took off the hood, wiping the water from his face.

"Forgive me, Shigeru," he said.

Shigeru smiled but did not speak. Summoning up his strength, he whispered my name.

"I'm here."

"Do you have Jato?"

"Yes, Lord Shigeru."

"Use it now. Take my head to Terayama and bury me

next to Takeshi." He paused as a fresh spasm of pain swept over him and then said, "And bring Iida's head to me there."

As Kenji helped him to kneel he said quietly, "Takeo has never failed me." I drew Jato from the scabbard. Shigeru stretched out his neck and murmured a few words: the prayers the Hidden use at the moment of death, followed by the name of the Enlightened One. I prayed, too, that I would not fail him now. It was darker than when Jato in his hand had saved my life.

I lifted the sword, felt the dull ache in my wrist, and asked Shigeru's forgiveness. The snake sword leaped and bit and, in its last act of service to its master, released him into the next world.

The silence of the night was utter. The gushing blood seemed monstrously loud. We took the head, bathed it in the river, and wrapped it in the hood, both dry-eyed, beyond grief or remorse.

There was a movement below the surface of the water, and seconds later Yuki surfaced like an otter. With her acute night vision she took in the scene, knelt by the body, and prayed briefly. I lifted the head—how heavy it was!—and put it in her hands.

"Take it to Terayama," I said. "I will meet you there."

She nodded, and I saw the slight flash of her teeth as she smiled.

"We must all leave now," Kenji hissed. "It was well done, but it's finished."

"First I must give his body to the river." I could not bear to leave it unburied on the bank. I took stones from the mouth of the canal and tied them into the loincloth that was his only garment. The others helped me carry him into the water.

I swam out to the deepest part of the river and let go, feeling the tug and drift as the body sank. Blood rose to the surface, dark against the white mist, but the river carried it away.

I thought of the house in Hagi where the river was always at the door and of the heron that came to the garden every evening. Now Otori Shigeru was dead. My tears flowed, and the river carried them away as well.

But for me the night's work was not finished. I swam back to the bank and picked up Jato. There was hardly a trace of blood on the blade. I wiped it and put it back in the scabbard. I knew Kenji was right—it would hamper my climbing—but I needed Jato now. I did not say a word to Kenji, and nothing to Yuki beyond "I'll see you in Terayama."

Kenji whispered, "Takeo," but without conviction. He must have known nothing would stop me. He embraced Yuki swiftly. It was only then that I realized that she was of course his daughter. He followed me back into the river.

· 6 ·

Kaede waited for night to come. She knew there was no other choice but to kill herself. She thought about dying with the same intensity she brought to everything. Her family's honor had depended on the marriage—so her father had told her. Now in the confusion and turmoil that had surrounded her all day, she clung to the conviction that the only way to protect her family's name was to act with honor herself.

It was early evening on what should have been her wedding day. She was still dressed in the robes that the Tohan ladies had prepared for her. They were more sumptuous and elegant than anything she had ever worn, and inside them she felt as tiny and fragile as a doll. The women's eyes had been red with weeping for the death of Lady Maruyama, but Kaede had been told nothing about this until after the massacre of the Otori men. Then one horror after another was revealed to her, until she thought she would go mad from outrage and grief.

The residence with its elegant rooms, its treasures of art, its beautiful gardens, had become a place of violence and torture. Outside its walls, across the nightingale floor, hung the man she was supposed to have married. All afternoon she had heard the guards, their taunts and their foul laughter. Her heart swelled to breaking point, and she wept constantly. Sometimes she heard her own name mentioned, and knew that her reputation had grown worse. She felt she had caused Lord Otori's downfall. She wept for him, for his utter humiliation at Iida's hands. She wept for her parents and the shame she was bringing on them.

Just when she thought she had cried her eyes dry, the tears welled and streamed down her face again. Lady Maruyama, Mariko, Sachie . . . they were all gone, swept away by the current of Tohan violence. All the people she cared about were either dead or vanished.

And she wept for herself because she was fifteen years

old and her life was over before it had begun. She mourned the husband she would never know, the children she would never bear, the future that the knife would put an end to. Her only consolation was the painting Takeo had given her. She held it in her hand and gazed on it constantly. Soon she would be free, like the little bird of the mountain.

Shizuka went to the kitchens for a while to ask for some food to be brought, joining in the guards' jokes with apparent heartlessness as she went past. When she returned the mask fell away. Her face was drawn with grief.

"Lady," she said, her bright voice belying her true feelings, "I must comb your hair. It's all over the place. And you must change your clothes."

She helped Kaede undress and called to the maids to take the heavy wedding robes away.

"I will put on my night robe now," Kaede said. "I will see no one else today."

Clad in the light cotton garment, she sat on the floor by the open window. It was raining gently and a little cooler. The garden dripped with moisture as though it, too, were in deepest mourning.

Shizuka knelt behind her, taking up the heavy weight of

her hair and running her fingers through it. She breathed into Kaede's ear, "I sent a message to the Muto residence in the city. I have just heard back from them. Takeo was hidden there, as I thought. They are going to permit him to retrieve Lord Otori's body."

"Lord Otori is dead?"

"No, not yet." Shizuka's voice trailed away. She was shaking with emotion. "The outrage," she murmured, "the shame. He cannot be left there. Takeo must come for him."

Kaede said, "Then he, too, will die today."

"My messenger is also going to try to reach Arai," Shizuka whispered. "But I do not know if he can arrive in time to help us."

"I never believed any one could challenge the Tohan," Kaede said. "Lord Iida is invincible. His cruelty gives him power." She gazed out of the window at the falling rain, the gray mist that enshrouded the mountains. "Why have men made such a harsh world?" she said in a low voice.

A string of wild geese flew overhead, calling mournfully. In the distance beyond the walls a deer barked.

Kaede put her hand to her head. Her hair was wet with Shizuka's tears. "When will Takeo come?"

"If he does, late at night." There was a long pause and then Shizuka said, "It is a hopeless venture."

Kaede did not reply. *I will wait for him,* she promised herself. *I will see him once more.*

She felt the cool handle of the knife inside her robe. Shizuka noticed the movement, drew her close, and embraced her. "Don't be afraid. Whatever you do, I will stay with you. I will follow you into the next world."

They held each other for a long time. Exhausted by emotion, Kaede slipped into the stage of bewilderment that accompanies grief. She felt as if she were dreaming and had entered another world, one in which she lay in Takeo's arms, without fear. *Only he can save me,* she found herself thinking. *Only he can bring me back to life.*

Later she told Shizuka she would like to bathe, and asked her to pluck her brow and eyebrows and scrub her feet and legs smooth. She ate a little and then sat in outwardly composed silence, meditating on what she had been taught as a child, remembering the serene face of the Enlightened One at Terayama.

"Have compassion on me," she prayed. "Help me to have courage."

The maids came to spread the beds. Kaede was getting ready to lie down and had placed the knife underneath the mattress. It was well into the hour of the Rat, and the residence had fallen silent, apart from the distant laughter of the guards, when they heard footsteps making the floor chirp. There was a tap on the door. Shizuka went to it and immediately dropped to the ground. Kaede heard Lord Abe's voice.

He has come to arrest Shizuka, she thought in terror.

Shizuka said, "It's very late, lord. Lady Shirakawa is exhausted," but Abe's voice was insistent. His footsteps retreated. Shizuka turned to Kaede and just had time to whisper, "Lord Iida wishes to visit you," before the floor sang again.

Iida stepped into the room, followed by Abe and the one-armed man, whose name she'd learned was Ando.

Kaede took one look at their faces, flushed with wine and with the triumph of their revenge. She dropped to the floor, her head pressed against the matting, her heart racing.

Iida settled himself down cross-legged. "Sit up, Lady Shirakawa."

She raised her head unwillingly and looked at him. He was casually dressed in nightclothes, but wore his sword in his sash. The two men who knelt behind him were also armed. They now sat up, too, studying Kaede with insulting curiosity.

"Forgive me for this late intrusion," Iida said, "but I felt the day should not end without me expressing my regrets for your unfortunate situation." He smiled at her, showing his big teeth, and said over his shoulder to Shizuka, "Leave."

Kaede's eyes widened and her breath came sharply, but she did not dare turn her head to look at Shizuka. She heard the door slide closed and guessed the girl would be somewhere close, on the other side. She sat without moving, eyes cast down, waiting for Iida to continue.

"Your marriage, which I thought was to form an alliance with the Otori, seems to have been the excuse for vipers to try to bite me. I think I have exterminated the nest, however." His eyes were fixed on her face. "You spent several weeks on the road with Otori Shigeru and Maruyama Nakomi. Did you never suspect they were plotting against me?"

"I knew nothing, lord," she said, and added quietly, "If there was a plot, it could only succeed with my ignorance."

"Unnh," he grunted, and after a long pause said, "Where is the young man?"

She had not thought her heart could beat more quickly,

but it did, pounding in her temples and making her faint. "Which young man, Lord Iida?"

"The so-called adopted son. Takeo."

"I know nothing of him," she replied, as if puzzled. "Why should I?"

"What kind of a man would you say he was?"

"He was young, very quiet. He seemed bookish; he liked to paint and draw." She forced herself to smile. "He was clumsy and . . . perhaps not very brave."

"That was Lord Abe's reading. We know now that he was one of the Hidden. He escaped execution a year ago. Why would Shigeru not only harbor but adopt a criminal like that, except to affront and insult me?"

Kaede could not answer. The webs of intrigue seemed unfathomable to her.

"Lord Abe believes the young man fled when Ando recognized him. It seems he is a coward. We'll pick him up sooner or later and I'll string him up next to his adopted father." Iida's eyes flickered over her, but she made no response. "Then my revenge on Shigeru will be complete." His teeth gleamed as he grinned. "However, a more pressing question is: What is to become of you? Come closer."

Kaede bowed and moved forward. Her heartbeat had slowed—indeed, seemed almost to have stopped. Time slowed too. The night became more silent. The rain was a gentle hiss. A cricket chirped.

Iida leaned forward and studied her. The lamplight fell on his face, and when she raised her eyes she saw his predatory features slacken with desire.

"I am torn, Lady Shirakawa. You are irretrievably tainted by these events, yet your father has been loyal to me, and I feel a certain responsibility towards you. What am I to do?"

"My only desire is to die," she replied. "Allow me to do so honorably. My father will be satisfied with that."

"Then there is the question of the Maruyama inheritance," he said. "I've thought of marrying you myself. That would deal with the problem of what happens to the domain, and would put an end to these rumors about your dangerous effect on men."

"The honor would be too great for me," she replied.

He smiled and ran one long fingernail across his front teeth. "I know you have two sisters. I may marry the older one. All in all, I think it is preferable if you take your own life."

"Lord Iida." She bowed to the ground.

"She's quite a wonderful girl, isn't she?" Iida said over his shoulder to the men behind him. "Beautiful, intelligent, brave. And all to be wasted."

She sat upright again, her face turned away from him, determined to show nothing to him.

"I suppose you are a virgin." He put out a hand and touched her hair. She realized he was far more drunk than he had appeared. She could smell the wine on his breath as he leaned towards her. To her fury, the touch made her tremble. He saw it and laughed. "It would be a tragedy to die a virgin. You should know at least one night of love."

Kaede stared at him in disbelief. She saw then all his depravity, how far he had descended into the pit of lust and cruelty. His great power had made him arrogant and corrupt. She felt as if she were in a dream, in which she could see what was going to happen but was powerless to prevent it. She could not believe his intentions.

He took her head in both hands and bent over her. She turned her face away, and his lips brushed her neck.

"No," she said. "No, lord. Do not shame me. Let me just die!"

"There is no shame in pleasing me," he said.

"I beseech you, not before these men," she cried, going limp as if she were surrendering to him. Her hair fell forward, covering her.

"Leave us," he said to them curtly. "Let no one disturb me before dawn."

She heard the two men leave, heard Shizuka speak to them, wanted to cry out, but did not dare. Iida knelt beside her, picked her up, and carried her to the mattress. He untied her girdle and her robe fell open. Removing his sword and loosening his own garments, he lay beside her. Her skin was crawling with fear and revulsion.

"We have all night," he said, the last words he spoke. The feel of his body pressing against her brought back vividly the guard at Noguchi Castle. His mouth on hers drove her nearly mad with disgust. She threw her arms back over her head, and he grunted in appreciation as her body arched against his. With her left hand she found the needle in her right sleeve. As he lowered himself onto her she drove the needle into his eye. He gave a cry, indistinguishable from a moan of passion. Pulling the knife from beneath the mattress with her right hand, she thrust it upwards. His own weight as he fell forward took it into his heart.

· 7 ·

I was soaked from the river and from the rain, water clinging to my hair and eyelashes, dripping like the rushes, like
bamboo and willow. And although it left no mark on my
dark clothes, I was soaked, too, with blood. The mist had
thickened even more. Kenji and I moved in a phantom world,
insubstantial and invisible. I found myself wondering if I had
died without knowing it and had come back as an angel of
revenge. When the night's work was done I would fade back
into the netherworld. And all the time grief was starting up its
terrible chanting in my heart, but I could not listen to it yet.

We came out of the moat and climbed the wall. I felt the
weight of Jato against my flank. It was as if I carried Shigeru

with me. I felt as if his ghost had entered me and had engraved itself on my bones. From the top of the garden wall I heard the steps of a patrol. Their voices were anxious; they suspected intruders, and when they saw the ropes that Yuki had cut, they stopped, exclaiming in surprise, and peering upwards to the iron rings where Shigeru had hung.

We took two each. They died in four strokes, before they could look down again. Shigeru had been right. The sword leaped in my hand as if it had a will of its own, or as if his own hand wielded it. No compassion or softness of mine hindered it.

The window above us was still open, and the lamp still burned faintly. The palace seemed quiet, wrapped in the sleep of the hour of the Ox. As we climbed inside we fell over the bodies of the guards Yuki had killed earlier. Kenji gave a faint approving sound. I went to the door between the corridor and the guardroom. I knew four such small rooms lay along the corridor. The first one was open and led into the antechamber where I had waited with Shigeru and we had looked at the paintings of the cranes. The other three were hidden behind the walls of Iida's apartments.

The nightingale floor ran around the whole residence

and through the middle, dividing the men's apartments from the women's. It lay before me, gleaming slightly in the lamp-light, silent.

I crouched in the shadows. From far away, almost at the end of the building, I could hear voices: two men at least, and a woman.

Shizuka.

After a few moments I realized the men were Abe and Ando; as for guards, I wasn't sure how many: perhaps two with the lords and ten or so others hidden in the secret compartments. I placed the voices in the end room, Iida's own. Presumably the lords were waiting for him there—but where was he and why was Shizuka with them?

Her voice was light, almost flirtatious, theirs tired, yawning, a little drunk.

"I'll fetch more wine," I heard her say.

"Yes, it looks like it's going to be a long night," Abe replied.

"One's last night on earth is always too short," Shizuka replied, a catch in her voice.

"It needn't be your last night, if you make the right move," Abe said, a heavy note of admiration creeping into his voice. "You're an attractive woman, and you know your way around. I'll make sure you're looked after."

"Lord Abe!" Shizuka laughed quietly. "Can I trust you?"

"Get some more wine and I'll show you how much."

I heard the floor sing as she stepped out of the room onto it. Heavier steps followed her, and Ando said, "I'm going to watch Shigeru dance again. I've waited a year for this."

As they moved through the middle of the residence I ran along the floor around the side and crouched by the door of the antechamber. The floor had stayed silent beneath my feet. Shizuka went past me, and Kenji gave his cricket chirp. She melted into the shadows.

Ando stepped into the antechamber and went to the guardroom. He called angrily to them to wake up, and then Kenji had him in a grip of iron. I went in, pulling off my hood, holding the lamp up so that he could see my face.

"Do you see me?" I whispered. "Do you know me? I am the boy from Mino. This is for my people. And for Lord Otori."

His eyes were filled with disbelief and fury. I would not use Jato on him. I took the garrote and killed him with that, while Kenji held him and Shizuka watched.

I whispered to her, "Where is Iida?"

She said, "With Kaede. In the farthest room on the women's side. I'll keep Abe quiet while you go around. He is alone with her. If there's any trouble here, I'll deal with it with Kenji."

I hardly took in her words. I'd thought my blood was cold, but now it turned to ice. I breathed deeply, let the Kikuta blackness rise in me and take me over completely, and ran out onto the nightingale floor.

Rain hissed gently in the garden beyond. Frogs croaked from the pools and the marshland. The women breathed deeply in sleep. I smelled the scent of flowers, the cypress wood of the bathhouse, the acrid stench from the privies. I floated across the floor as weightless as a ghost. Behind me the castle loomed, in front of me flowed the river. Iida was waiting for me.

In the last small room at the end of the residence, a lamp burned. The wooden shutters were open but the paper ones closed, and against the orange glow of the lamp I could see the shadow of a woman sitting motionless, her hair falling around her.

With Jato ready, I pulled the screen open and leaped into the room.

Kaede, sword in hand, was on her feet in a moment. She was covered in blood.

Iida lay slumped on the mattress, facedown. Kaede said, "It's best to kill a man and take his sword. That's what Shizuka said."

Her eyes were dilated with shock, and she was trembling. There was something almost supernatural about the scene: the girl, so young and frail; the man, massive and powerful, even in death; the hiss of the rain; the stillness of the night. . . .

I put Jato down. She lowered Iida's sword and stepped towards me. "Takeo," she said, as if awakening from a dream. "He tried to . . . I killed him. . . ."

Then she was in my arms. I held her until she stopped shaking.

"You're soaking wet," she whispered. "Aren't you cold?"

I had not been, but now I was, shivering almost as much as she was. Iida was dead, but I had not killed him. I felt cheated of my revenge, but I could not argue with fate, which had dealt with him through Kaede's hands. I was both disappointed and mad with relief. And I was holding Kaede, as I had longed to for weeks.

When I think about what happened next, I can only plead that we were bewitched, as we had been since Tsuwano. Kaede said, "I expected to die tonight."

"I think we will," I said.

"But we will be together," she breathed against my ear. "No one will come here before dawn."

Her voice, her touch, set me aching with love and desire for her.

"Do you want me?" she said.

"You know I do." We fell to our knees, still holding each other.

"You aren't afraid of me? Of what happens to men because of me?"

"No. You will never be dangerous to me. Are you afraid?"

"No," she said, with a kind of wonder in her voice. "I want to be with you before we die." Her mouth found mine. She undid her girdle and her robe fell open. I pulled my wet clothes off and felt against me the skin I had longed for. Our bodies rushed towards each other with the urgency and madness of youth.

I would have been happy to die afterwards, but like the

river, life dragged us forward. It seemed an eternity had passed, but it could have been no more than fifteen minutes, for I heard the floor sing and heard Shizuka return to Abe. In the room next to us a woman said something in her sleep, following it with a bitter laugh that set the hairs upright on my neck.

"What's Ando doing?" Abe said.

"He fell asleep," Shizuka replied, giggling. "He can't hold his wine like Lord Abe."

The liquid gurgled from flask to bowl. I heard Abe swallow. I touched my lips to Kaede's eyelids and hair. "I must go back to Kenji," I whispered. "I can't leave him and Shizuka unprotected."

"Why don't we just die together now," she said, "while we are happy?"

"He came on my account," I replied. "If I can save his life, I must."

"I'll come with you." She stood swiftly and retied her robe, taking up the sword again. The lamp was guttering, almost extinguished. In the distance I heard the first cock crow from the town.

"No. Stay here while I go back for Kenji. We'll meet you

here and escape through the garden. Can you swim?"

She shook her head. "I never learned. But there are boats on the moat. Perhaps we can take one of them."

I pulled on my wet clothes again, shuddering at their clamminess against my skin. When I took up Jato, I felt the ache in my wrist. One of the blows of the night must have jarred it again. I knew I had to take Iida's head now, so I told Kaede to stretch out his neck by his hair. She did so, flinching a little.

"This is for Shigeru," I whispered as Jato sliced through his neck. He had already bled profusely, so there was no great gush of blood. I cut his robe and wrapped the head in it. It was as heavy as Shigeru's had been when I handed it to Yuki. I could not believe it was still the same night. I left the head on the floor, embraced Kaede one last time, and went back the way I had come.

Kenji was still in the guardroom, and I could hear Shizuka chuckling with Abe. He whispered, "The next patrol is due any minute. They're going to find the bodies."

"It's done," I said. "Iida is dead."

"Then let's go."

"I have to deal with Abe."

"Leave him to Shizuka."

"And we have to take Kaede with us."

He peered at me in the gloom. "Lady Shirakawa? Are you mad?"

Very likely I was. I did not answer him. Instead, I stepped heavily and deliberately onto the nightingale floor.

It cried out immediately. Abe called, "Who's there?"

He rushed out of the room, his robe loose, sword in his hand. Behind him came two guards, one of them holding a torch. In its light Abe saw me, and recognized me. His expression was first astonished, then scornful. He strode towards me, making the floor sing loudly. Behind him Shizuka leaped at one of the guards and cut his throat. The other turned in amazement, dropping the torch as he drew his sword.

Abe was shouting for help. He came towards me like a madman, the great sword in his hand. He cut at me and I parried it, but his strength was huge, and my arm weakened by pain. I ducked under his second blow and went invisible briefly. I was taken aback by his ferocity and skill.

Kenji was alongside me, but now the rest of the guards came pouring from their hiding places. Shizuka dealt with two of them; Kenji left his second self below the sword of one, and then knifed him in the back. My attention was totally taken up with Abe, who was driving me down the nightingale floor towards the end of the building. The women had woken and ran out screaming, distracting Abe as they fled past him and giving me a moment to recover my breath. I knew we could deal with the guards, once I had got Abe out of the way. But at the same time I knew he was vastly more skillful and experienced than I was.

He was driving me into the corner of the building, where there was no room to evade him. I went invisible again, but he knew there was nowhere for me to go. Whether I was invisible or not, his sword could still cut me in two.

Then, when it seemed he had me, he faltered and his mouth fell open. He gazed over my shoulder, a look of horror on his face.

I did not follow his look, but in that moment of inattention drove Jato downwards. The sword fell from my hands as my right arm gave. Abe lurched forward, his brains bursting from the great split in his skull. I ducked out of the way and turned to see Kaede standing in the doorway, the lamp behind her. In one hand she held Iida's sword, in the other his head.

Side by side we fought our way back across the nightingale floor. Every stroke made me wince in pain. Without Kaede at my right side, I would have died then.

Everything was turning blurred and indistinct before my eyes. I thought the mist from the river had penetrated the residence, but then I heard crackling and smelled smoke. The torch the guard had dropped had set the wooden screens on fire.

There were cries of fear and shock. The women and servants were running from the fire, out of the residence and into the castle, while guards from the castle were trying to get through the narrow gate into the residence. In the confusion and the smoke, the four of us fought our way into the garden.

By now the residence was fully ablaze. No one knew where Iida was or if he was alive or dead. No one knew who had made this attack on the supposedly impregnable castle. Was it men or demons? Shigeru had been spirited away. Was it by men or angels?

The rain had eased, but the mist grew thicker as dawn approached. Shizuka led us through the garden to the gate and the steps down to the moat. The guards here had already started on their way up towards the residence. Distracted and confused as they were, they hardly put up a fight. We unbarred the gate easily from the inside and stepped into one of the boats, casting off the rope.

The moat was connected to the river through the marshland we had crossed earlier. Behind us the castle stood out stark against the flames. Ash floated towards us, falling on our hair. The river was surging, and the waves rocked the wooden pleasure boat as the current carried us into it. It was hardly more than a punt, and I feared if the water grew any wilder it would capsize. Ahead of us the piles of the bridge suddenly appeared. For a moment I thought we would be flung against them, but the boat dived through, nose first, and the river carried us on, past the town.

None of us said much. We were all breathing hard, charged with the near confrontation with death, subdued maybe by the memory of those we had sent on into the next world, but deeply, achingly glad we were not among them. At least, that was how I felt.

I went to the stern of the boat and took the oar, but the current was too strong to make any headway. We had to go where it took us. The mist turned white as dawn came, but we could see no more through it than when it had been dark.

Apart from the glow of the flames from the castle, everything else had disappeared.

I was aware of a strange noise, however, above the song of the river. It was like a great humming, as though a huge swarm of insects were descending on the city.

"Can you hear that?" I said to Shizuka.

She was frowning. "What is it?"

"I don't know."

The sun brightened, burning off the haze. The hum and throb from the bank increased, until the sound resolved itself into something I suddenly recognized: the tramp of feet of thousands of men and horses, the jingle of harness, the clash of steel. Colors flashed at us through the torn shreds of mist; the crests and banners of the western clans.

"Arai is here!" Shizuka cried.

There are chronicles enough of the fall of Inuyama, and I took no further part in it, so there is no need for me to describe it here.

I had not expected to live beyond that night. I had no idea what to do next. I had given my life to the Tribe, that much was clear to me, but I still had duties to perform for Shigeru.

Kaede knew nothing of my bargain with the Kikuta. If I were Otori, Shigeru's heir, it would be my duty to marry her, and indeed there was nothing I wanted more. If I were to become Kikuta, Lady Shirakawa would be as unobtainable as the moon. What had happened between us now seemed like a dream. If I thought about it, I felt I should be ashamed of what I had done, and so like a coward I put it out of my mind.

We went first to the Muto residence where I had been hidden, changed our clothes, grabbed a little food. Shizuka went immediately to speak to Arai, leaving Kaede in the charge of the women of the house.

I did not want to speak to Kenji, or anyone. I wanted to get to Terayama, bury Shigeru, and place Iida's head on the grave. I knew I had to do this quickly, before the Kikuta controlled me fully. I was aware that I had already disobeyed the master of my family by returning to the castle. Even though I had not killed Iida myself, everyone would assume I had, against the express wishes of the Tribe. I could not deny it without causing immense harm to Kaede. I did not intend to disobey forever. I just needed a little more time.

It was easy enough to slip out of the house during the confusion of that day. I went to the lodging house where I had stayed with Shigeru. The owners had fled before Arai's army, taking most of their possessions with them, but many of our things were still in the rooms, including the sketches I had done at Terayama, and the writing box on which Shigeru had written his final letter to me. I looked at them with sorrow. Grief's clamor was growing louder and louder inside me, demanding my attention. It seemed I could feel Shigeru's presence in the room, see him sitting in the open doorway as night fell and I did not return.

I did not take much: a change of clothes, a little money, and my horse, Raku, from the stables. Shigeru's black, Kyu, had disappeared, as had most of the Otori horses, but Raku was still there, restive and uneasy as the smell of fire drifted over the town. He was relieved to see me. I saddled him up, tied the basket that held Iida's head to the saddle bow, and rode out of the city, joining the throngs of people on the highway who were fleeing from the approaching armies.

I went swiftly, sleeping only a little at night. The weather had cleared, and the air was crisp with a hint of autumn.

Each day the mountains rose clear-edged against a brilliant blue sky. Some of the trees were already showing golden leaves. Bush clover and arrowroot were beginning to flower. It was probably beautiful, but I saw no beauty in anything. I knew I had to reflect on what I would do, but I could not bear to look at what I had done. I was in that stage of grief where I could not bear to go forward. I only wanted to go back, back to the house in Hagi, back in time to when Shigeru was alive, before we left for Inuyama.

On the afternoon of the fourth day, when I had just passed Kushimoto, I became aware that the travelers on the road were now streaming towards me. I called to a farmer leading a packhorse, "What's up ahead?"

"Monks! Warriors!" he shouted back. "Yamagata has fallen to them. The Tohan are fleeing. They say Lord Iida is dead!"

I grinned, wondering what he would do if he saw the grisly baggage on my saddle. I was in traveling clothes, unmarked with any crest. No one knew who I was, and I did not know that my name had already become famous.

Before long I heard the sound of men at arms on the road ahead, and I took Raku into the forest. I did not want to lose him or get embroiled in petty fights with the retreating Tohan. They were moving fast, obviously hoping to reach Inuyama before the monks caught up with them, but I felt they would be held up at the pass at Kushimoto and would probably have to make a stand there.

They straggled past for most of the rest of the day, while I worked my way northward through the forest, avoiding them as often as I could, though twice I had to use Jato to defend myself and my horse. My wrist still bothered me, and as the sun set I became more uneasy—not for my own safety, but that my mission would not be accomplished. It seemed too dangerous to try to sleep. The moon was bright, and I rode all night beneath its light, Raku moving on with his easy stride, one ear forward, one back.

Dawn came and I saw in the distance the shape of the mountains that surrounded Terayama. I would be there before the end of the day. I saw a pool below the road, and stopped to let Raku drink. The sun rose, and in its warmth I became suddenly sleepy. I tied the horse to a tree and took the saddle for a pillow, lay down, and fell immediately asleep.

I was woken by the earth shaking beneath me. I lay for a moment, looking at the dappled light that fell on the pool, listening to the trickle of the water and the tread of hundreds of feet approaching along the road. I stood, meaning to take Raku deeper into the forest to hide him, but when I looked up I saw that the army was not the last of the Tohan. The men wore armor and carried weapons, but the banners were of the Otori, and of the temple at Terayama. Those that did not wear helmets had shaven heads, and in the front rank I recognized the young man who had shown us the paintings.

"Makoto!" I called to him, climbing the bank towards him. He turned to me, and a look of joy and astonishment crossed his face.

"Lord Otori? Is it really you? We feared you would be dead too. We are riding to avenge Lord Shigeru."

"I am on my way to Terayama," I said. "I am taking Iida's head to him, as he commanded me."

His eyes widened a little. "Iida is already dead?"

"Yes, and Inuyama has fallen to Arai. You'll catch up with the Tohan at Kushimoto."

"Won't you ride with us?"

I stared at him. His words made no sense to me. My work was almost done. I had to finish my last duty to Shigeru, and then I would disappear into the secret world of the Tribe. But of course there was no way Makoto could know of the choices I had made.

"Are you all right?" he asked. "You're not wounded?"

I shook my head. "I have to place the head on Shigeru's grave."

Makoto's eyes gleamed. "Show it to us!"

I brought the basket and opened it. The smell was strengthening and flies had gathered on the blood. The skin was a waxy gray color, the eyes dull and bloodshot.

Makoto took it by the topknot, leaped onto a boulder by the side of the road, and held it up to the monks gathered around. "Now see what Lord Otori has done!" he shouted, and the men shouted back a great hurrah. A wave of emotion swept through them. I heard my name repeated over and over again as, one by one at first, and then as if with a single mind, they knelt in the dust before me, bowing to the ground.

Kenji was right: People had loved Shigeru—the monks, the farmers, most of the Otori clan—and because I had carried out the revenge, that love was transferred to me.

It seemed to add to my burdens. I did not want this adulation. I did not deserve it, and I was in no position to live up to it. I bade farewell to the monks, wished them success, and rode on, the head back in its basket.

They did not want me to go alone, and so Makoto came with me. He told me how Yuki had arrived at Terayama with Shigeru's head, and they were preparing the burial rites. She must have traveled day and night to get there so soon, and I thought of her with enormous gratitude.

By evening we were in the temple. Led by the old priest, the monks who remained there were chanting the sutras for Shigeru, and the stone had already been erected over the place where the head was buried. I knelt by it and placed his enemy's head before him. The moon was half-full. In its ethereal light the rocks in the Sesshu garden looked like men praying. The sound of the waterfall seemed louder than by day. Beneath it I could hear the cedars sighing as the night breeze stirred them. Crickets shrilled and frogs were croaking from the pools below the cascade. I heard the beating of wings, and saw the shy hawk owl swoop through the graveyard. Soon it would migrate again; soon summer would be over.

I thought it was a beautiful place for his spirit to rest in. I stayed by the grave for a long time, tears flowing silently. He had told me that only children cry. Men endure, he said, but what seemed unthinkable to me was that I should be the man who would take his place. I was haunted by the conviction that I should not have dealt the deathblow. I had beheaded him with his own sword. I was not his heir: I was his murderer.

I thought longingly of the house in Hagi, with its song of the river and the world. I wanted it to sing that song to my children. I wanted them to grow up beneath its gentle shelter. I daydreamed that Kaede would prepare tea in the room Shigeru built, and our children would try to outwit the nightingale floor. In the evenings we would watch the heron come to the garden, its great gray shape standing patiently in the stream.

In the depths of the garden someone was playing the flute. Its liquid notes pierced my heart. I did not think I would ever recover from my grief.

The days passed, and I could not leave the temple. I knew I must make a decision and leave, but each day I put it off. I was aware that the old priest and Makoto were concerned for me, but they left me alone, apart from looking after me in practical ways, reminding me to eat, to bathe, to sleep.

Every day people came to pray at Shigeru's grave. At first a trickle, then a flood, of returning soldiers, monks, farmers, and peasants filed reverently past the tombstone, prostrating themselves before it, their faces wet with tears. Shigeru had been right: He was even more powerful, and more beloved, in death than in life.

"He will become a god," the old priest predicted. "He will join the others in the shrine."

Night after night I dreamed of Shigeru as I had last seen him, his features streaked with water and blood, and when I woke, my heart pounding with horror, I heard the flute. I began to look forward to the mournful notes as I lay sleepless. I found its music both painful and consoling.

The moon waned; the nights were darker. We heard of the victory at Kushimoto from the returning monks. Life at the temple began to return to normal, the old rituals closing like water over the heads of the dead. Then word came that Lord Arai, who was now master of most of the Three Countries, was coming to Terayama to pay his respects to Shigeru's grave.

That night, when I heard the flute music, I went to talk to the player. It was, as I had half-suspected, Makoto. I was deeply touched that he should have been watching over me, accompanying me in my sorrow.

He was sitting by the pool, where sometimes in the day I had seen him feed the golden carp. He finished the phrase and laid the flute down.

"You will have to come to a decision once Arai is here," he said. "What will you do?"

I sat down next to him. The dew was falling, and the stones were wet. "What should I do?"

"You are Shigeru's heir. You must take up his inheritance." He paused, then said, "But it is not that simple, is it? There is something else that calls you."

"It doesn't exactly call me. It commands me. I am under an obligation. . . . It's hard to explain it to anyone."

"Try me," he said.

"You know I have acute hearing. Like a dog, you once said."

"I shouldn't have said that. It hurt you. Forgive me."

"No, you were right. 'Useful to your masters,' you said. Well, I am useful to my masters, and they are not the Otori."

"The Tribe?"

"You know of them?"

"Only a little," he said. "Our abbot mentioned them."

There was a moment when I thought he was going to say

something else, that he was waiting for me to ask a question. But I did not know the right question to ask then, and I was too absorbed in my own thoughts, and my own need to explain them.

"My father was of the Tribe, and the talents I have come from him. They have claimed me, as they believe they have the right. I made a bargain with them that they would allow me to rescue Lord Shigeru, and in return I would join them."

"What right do they have to demand that of you, when you are Shigeru's legal heir?" he asked, indignant.

"If I try to escape from them, they will kill me," I replied. "They believe they have that right, and as I made the bargain, I believe it too. My life is theirs."

"You must have made the agreement under duress," he said. "No one will expect you to keep it. You are Otori Takeo. I don't think you realize how famous you have become, how much your name means."

"I killed him," I said, and to my shame felt the tears begin to flow again. "I can never forgive myself. I can't take on his name and his life. He died at my hands."

"You gave him an honorable death," Makoto whispered, taking my hands in his. "You fulfilled every duty a son should to his father. Everywhere you are admired and praised for it. And to kill Iida too. It is the stuff of legends."

"I have not fulfilled every duty," I replied. "His uncles plotted his death with Iida, and they go unpunished. And he charged me to take care of Lady Shirakawa, who has suffered terribly through no fault of her own."

"That would not be too much of a burden," he said, eyeing me ironically, and I felt the blood rise in my face. "I noticed your hands touching," he said, and after a pause: "I notice everything about you."

"I want to fulfill his wishes, yet I feel unworthy. And anyway, I am bound by my oath to the Tribe."

"That could be broken, if you wanted."

Maybe Makoto was right. On the other hand, maybe the Tribe would not let me live. And besides, I could not hide it from myself: Something in me was drawn to them. I kept recalling how I'd felt Kikuta had understood my nature, and how that nature had responded to the dark skills of the Tribe. I was all too aware of the deep divisions within me. I wanted to open my heart to Makoto, but to do so would mean telling him everything, and I could not talk about being born into the Hidden to a monk who was a follower of the

Enlightened One. I thought of how I had now broken all the commandments. I had killed many times.

While we spoke in whispers in the darkened garden, the silence broken only by the sudden splash of a fish or the distant hooting of owls, the feeling between us had grown more intense. Now Makoto drew me into his embrace and held me closely. "Whatever you choose, you must let go of your grief," he said. "You did the best you could. Shigeru would have been proud of you. Now you have to forgive, and be proud of, yourself."

His affectionate words, his touch, made the tears flow again. Beneath his hands I felt my body come back to life. He drew me back from the abyss and made me desire to live again. Afterwards, I slept deeply, and did not dream.

Arai came with a few retainers and twenty or so men, leaving the bulk of his army to maintain the peace in the East. He meant to ride on and settle the borders before winter came. He had never been patient; now he was driven. He was younger than Shigeru, about twenty-six, in the prime of manhood, a big man with a quick temper and an iron will.

I did not want him as an enemy, and he made no secret of the fact that he wanted me as an ally and would support me against the Otori lords. Moreover, he had already decided that I should marry Kaede.

He had brought her with him, as custom dictated she should visit Shigeru's grave. He thought we should both stay at the temple while arrangements were made for the marriage. Shizuka of course accompanied her and found an opportunity to speak privately to me.

"I knew we'd find you here," she said. "The Kikuta have been furious, but my uncle persuaded them to give you a little more leeway. Your time's running out, though."

"I am ready to go to them," I replied.

"They will come for you tonight."

"Does Lady Shirakawa know?"

"I have tried to warn her, and I have tried to warn Arai." Shizuka's voice was heavy with frustration.

For Arai had very different plans. "You are Shigeru's legal heir," he said as we sat in the guest room of the temple, after he had paid his respects to the grave. "It's entirely fitting that you marry Lady Shirakawa. We will secure Maruyama for her, and then turn our attention to the Otori next spring. I need an ally in Hagi." He was scrutinizing my face. "I don't mind telling you, your reputation makes you a desirable one."

"Lord Arai is too generous," I replied. "However, there are other considerations that may prevent me from complying with your wishes."

"Don't be a fool," he said shortly. "I believe my wishes and yours mesh very well together."

My mind had gone empty: My thoughts had all taken flight like Sesshu's birds. I knew Shizuka would be listening from outside. Arai had been Shigeru's ally; he had protected Kaede; now he had conquered most of the Three Countries. If I owed anyone allegiance, it was to him. I did not think I could just disappear without giving him some explanation.

"Anything I achieved was with the help of the Tribe," I said slowly.

A flicker of anger crossed his face, but he did not speak.

"I made a pact with them, and to keep my side of it, I must give up the Otori name and go with them."

"Who are the Tribe?" he exploded. "Everywhere I turn I run into them. They are like rats in the grain store. Even those closest to me . . . !"

"We could not have defeated Iida without their help," I said.

He shook his large head and sighed. "I don't want to hear this nonsense. You were adopted by Shigeru, you are Otori, you will marry Lady Shirakawa. That is my command."

"Lord Arai." I bowed to the ground, fully aware that I could not obey him.

After visiting the grave, Kaede had returned to the women's guest house and I had no chance to speak to her. I longed to see her but also feared it. I was afraid of her power over me, and mine over her. I was afraid of hurting her and, worse, of not daring to hurt her. That night, sleepless, I went again and sat in the garden, longing for silence but always listening. I knew I would go with Kikuta when he came for me that night, but I could not rid my mind of the image and memory of Kaede, the sight of her next to Iida's body, the feel of her skin against mine, her frailty as I entered her. The idea of never feeling that again was so painful, it took the breath from my lungs.

I heard the soft tread of a woman's feet. Shizuka placed her hand, so like mine in shape and design, on my shoulder and whispered, "Lady Shirakawa wishes to see you."

"I must not," I replied.

"They will be here before dawn," Shizuka said. "I have told her they will never relinquish their claim on you. In fact, because of your disobedience in Inuyama, the master has already decided that if you do not go with them tonight, you will die. She wants to say good-bye."

I followed her. Kaede was sitting at the far end of the veranda, her figure lit dimly by the setting moon. I thought I would recognize her outline anywhere, the shape of her head, the set of her shoulders, the characteristic movement as she turned her face towards me.

The moonlight glinted on her eyes, making them like pools of black mountain water when the snow covers the land and the world is all white and gray. I dropped on my knees before her. The silvery wood smelled of the forest and the shrine, of sap and incense.

"Shizuka says you must leave me, that we cannot be married." Her voice was low and bewildered.

"The Tribe will not allow me to lead that life. I am not—can never now be—a lord of the Otori clan."

"But Arai will protect you. It's what he wants. Nothing need stand in our way."

"I made a deal with the man who is the master of my family," I said. "My life is his from now on."

In that moment, in the silence of the night, I thought of my father, who had tried to escape his blood destiny and had been murdered for it. I did not think my sadness could be any deeper, but this thought dredged out a new level.

Kaede said, "In eight years as a hostage I never asked anyone for anything. Iida Sadamu ordered me to kill myself: I did not plead with him. He was going to rape me: I did not beg for mercy. But I am asking you now: Don't leave me. I am begging you to marry me. I will never ask anyone for anything again."

She threw herself to the ground before me, her hair and her robe touching the floor with a silky hiss. I could smell her perfume. Her hair was so close, it brushed my hands.

"I'm afraid," she whispered. "I'm afraid of myself. I am only safe with you."

It was even more painful than I had anticipated. And what made it worse was the knowledge that if we could just lie together, skin against skin, all pain would cease.

"The Tribe will kill me," I said finally.

"There are worse things than death! If they kill you, I

will kill myself and follow you." She took my hands in hers and leaned towards me. Her eyes were burning, her hands dry and hot, the bones as fragile as a bird's. I could feel the blood racing beneath the skin. "If we can't live together we should die together."

Her voice was urgent and excited. The night air seemed suddenly chill. In songs and romances, couples died together for love. I remembered Kenji's words to Shigeru: *You are in love with death, like all your class.* Kaede was of the same class and background, but I was not. I did not want to die. I was not yet eighteen years old.

My silence was enough answer for her. Her eyes searched my face. "I will never love anyone but you," she said.

It seemed we had hardly ever looked directly at each other. Our glances had always been stolen and indirect. Now that we were parting, we could gaze into each other's eyes, beyond modesty or shame. I could feel her pain and her despair. I wanted to ease her suffering, but I could not do what she asked. Out of my confusion, as I held her hands and stared deeply into her eyes, some power came. Her gaze intensified as if she were drowning. Then she sighed and her eyes closed. Her body swayed. Shizuka leaped forward from the shadows and caught her as she fell. Together we lowered her carefully to the floor. She was deeply asleep, as I had been under Kikuta's eyes in the hidden room.

I shivered, suddenly terribly cold.

"You should not have done that," Shizuka whispered.

I knew my cousin was right. "I did not mean to," I said. "I've never done it to a human being before. Only to dogs."

She slapped me on the arm. "Go to the Kikuta. Go and learn to control your skills. Maybe you'll grow up there."

"Will she be all right?"

"I don't know about these Kikuta things," Shizuka said.

"I slept for twenty-four hours."

"Presumably, whoever put you to sleep knew what they were doing," she retorted.

From far away down the mountain path I could hear people approaching: two men walking quietly, but not quietly enough for me.

"They're coming," I said.

Shizuka knelt beside Kaede and lifted her with her easy strength. "Good-bye, Cousin," she said, her voice still angry.

"Shizuka . . ." I began as she walked towards the room. She stopped for a moment but did not turn.

221

"My horse, Raku—will you see Lady Shirakawa takes him?" I had nothing else to give her.

Shizuka nodded and moved away into the shadows, out of my sight. I heard the door slide, her tread on the matting, the faint creak of the floor as she laid Kaede down.

I went back to my room and gathered together my belongings. I owned nothing, really: the letter from Shigeru, my knife, and Jato. Then I went to the temple, where Makoto knelt in meditation. I touched him on the shoulder, and he rose and came outside with me.

"I'm leaving," I whispered. "Don't tell anyone before morning."

"You could stay here."

"It's not possible."

"Come back then when you can. We can hide you here. There are so many secret places in the mountains. No one would ever find you."

"Maybe I'll need that one day," I replied. "I want you to keep my sword for me."

He took Jato. "Now I know you'll be back." He put out his hand and traced the outline of my mouth, the edge of bone beneath my cheek, the nape of my neck.

I was light-headed with lack of sleep, with grief and desire. I wanted to lie down and be held by someone, but the footsteps were crossing the gravel now.

"Who's there?" Makoto turned, the sword ready in his hand. "Shall I rouse the temple?"

"No! These are the people I must go with. Lord Arai must not know."

The two of them, my former teacher Muto Kenji and the Kikuta master, waited in the moonlight. They were in traveling clothes, unremarkable, rather impoverished, two brothers perhaps, scholars or unsuccessful merchants. You had to know them as I did to see the alert stance, the hard line of muscle that spoke of their great physical strength, the ears and eyes that missed nothing, the supreme intelligence that made warlords like Iida and Arai seem brutal and clumsy.

I dropped to the ground before the Kikuta master and bowed my head to the dust.

"Stand up, Takeo," he said, and to my surprise both he and Kenji embraced me.

Makoto clasped my hands. "Farewell. I know we'll meet again. Our lives are bound together."

"Show me Lord Shigeru's grave," Kikuta said to me gently, in the way I remembered: as one who understood my true nature.

But for you he would not be in it, I thought, but I did not speak it. In the peace of the night I began to accept that it was Shigeru's fate to die the way he did, just as it was his fate now to become a god, a hero to many people, who would come here to the shrine to pray to him, to seek his help, for hundreds of years to come, as long as Terayama stood— maybe forever.

We stood with bowed heads before the newly carved stone. Who knows what Kenji and Kikuta said in their hearts? I asked Shigeru's forgiveness, thanked him again for saving my life in Mino, and bade him farewell. I thought I heard his voice and saw his openhearted smile.

The wind stirred the ancient cedars; the night insects kept up their insistent music. It would always be like this, I thought, summer after summer, winter after winter, the moon sinking towards the West, giving the night back to the stars, and they, in an hour or two, surrendering it to the brightness of the sun.

The sun would pass above the mountains, pulling the

shadows of the cedars after it, until it descended again below the rim of the hills. So the world went, and humankind lived on it as best they could, between the darkness and the light.

ACKNOWLEDGMENTS

The main characters, Takeo and Kaede, came into my head on my first trip to Japan in 1993. Many people have helped me research and realize their story. I would like to thank the Asialink Foundation, who awarded me a fellowship in 1999 to spend three months in Japan, the Australia Council, the Department of Trade and Foreign Affairs and the Australian Embassy in Tokyo, and ArtsSA, the South Australian Government Arts Department. In Japan I was sponsored by Yamaguchi Prefecture's Akiyoshidai International Arts Village whose staff gave me invaluable help in exploring the landscape and the history of Western Honshuu. I would particularly like to thank Mr. Kori Yoshinori, Ms. Matsunaga Yayoi, and Ms. Matsubara Manami. I am especially grateful to Mrs. Tokorigi Masako for showing me the Sesshu paintings and gardens and to her husband, Miki, for information on horses in the medieval period.

Spending time in Japan with two theater companies gave me many insights—deepest thanks to Kazenoko in Tokyo and Kyushuu and Gekidan Urinko in Nagoya, and to Ms. Kimura Miyo, a wonderful traveling companion, who accompanied me to Kanazawa and the Nakasendo and who has answered many questions for me about language and literature.

I thank Mr. Mogi Masaru and Mrs. Mogi Akiko for their help with research, their suggestions for names, and, above all, their ongoing friendship.

In Australia I would like to thank my two Japanese teachers, Mrs. Thuy Coombes and Mrs. Etsuko Wilson; Simon Higgins, who made some invaluable suggestions; my agent, Jenny Darling; my son Matt, my first reader on all three books; and the rest of my family for not only putting up with but sharing my obsessions.

I would also like to acknowledge the insights and expert knowledge of the samurai history archive on the World Wide Web and members of the discussion forum.

Calligraphy was drawn for me by Ms. Sugiyama Kazuko and Etsuko Wilson. I am immensely grateful to them.

Turn the page for a preview of

Grass for his Pillow

EPISODE 1

· 1 ·

Shirakawa Kaede lay deeply asleep in the state close to unconsciousness that the Kikuta can deliver with their gaze. The night passed, the stars paled as dawn came, the sounds of the temple rose and fell around her, but she did not stir. She did not hear her companion, Shizuka, call anxiously to her from time to time, trying to wake her. She did not feel Shizuka's hand on her forehead. She did not hear Lord Arai Daiichi's men as they came with increasing impatience to the veranda, telling Shizuka that the warlord was waiting to speak to Lady Shirakawa. Her breathing was peaceful and calm, her features as still as a mask's.

Toward evening the quality of her sleep seemed to change.

Her eyelids flickered and her lips appeared to smile. Her fingers, which had been curled gently against her palms, spread.

Be patient. He will come for you.

Kaede was dreaming that she had been turned to ice. The words echoed lucidly in her head. There was no fear in the dream, just the feeling of being held by something cool and white in a world that was silent, frozen, and enchanted.

Her eyes opened.

It was still light. The shadows told her it was evening. A wind bell rang softly, once, and then the air was still. The day she had no recollection of must have been a warm one. Her skin was damp beneath her hair. Birds were chattering from the eaves, and she could hear the clip of the swallows' beaks as they caught the last insects of the day. Soon they would fly south. It was already autumn.

The sound of the birds reminded her of the painting Takeo had given her, many weeks before, at this same place, a sketch of a wild forest bird that had made her think of freedom; it had been lost along with everything else she possessed, her wedding robes, all her other clothes, when the castle at Inuyama burned. She possessed nothing. Shizuka had found some old robes for her at the house they had stayed in, and had borrowed combs and other things. She had never been in such a place before, a merchant's house, smelling of fermenting soy, full of people, whom she tried to keep away from, though every now and then the maids came to peep at her through the screens.

She was afraid everyone would see what had happened to her on the night the castle fell. She had killed a man, she had lain with another, she had fought alongside him, wielding the dead man's sword. She could not believe she had done these things. Sometimes she thought she was bewitched, as people said. They said of her that any man who desired her died—and it was true. Men had died. But not Takeo.

Ever since she had been assaulted by the guard when she was a hostage in Noguchi Castle, she had been afraid of all men. Her terror of Iida had driven her to defend herself against him, but she had had no fear of Takeo. She had only wanted to hold him closer. Since their first meeting in Tsuwano, her body had longed for his. She had wanted him to touch her, she had wanted the feel of his skin against hers. Now, as she remembered that night, she understood with

3

renewed clarity that she could marry no one but him, she would love no one but him. *I will be patient*, she promised. But where had those words come from?

She turned her head slightly and saw Shizuka's outline on the edge of the veranda. Beyond the woman rose the ancient trees of the shrine. The air smelled of cedars and dust. The temple bell tolled the evening hour. Kaede did not speak. She did not want to talk to anyone, or hear any voice. She wanted to go back to that place of ice where she had been sleeping.

Then, beyond the specks of dust that floated in the last rays of the sun, she saw something: a spirit, she thought, yet not only a spirit, for it had substance; it was there, undeniable and real, gleaming like fresh snow. She stared, half rose, but in the moment that she recognized her, the White Goddess, the all-compassionate, the all-merciful, was gone.

"What is it?" Shizuka heard the movement and ran to her side. Kaede looked at Shizuka and saw the deep concern in her eyes. She realized how precious this woman had become to her—her closest, indeed her only friend.

"Nothing. A half-dream."

"Are you all right? How do you feel?"

"I don't know. I feel . . ." Kaede's voice died away. She gazed at Shizuka for several moments. "Have I been asleep all day? What happened to me?"

"He shouldn't have done it to you," Shizuka said, her voice sharp with concern and anger.

"It was Takeo?"

Shizuka nodded. "I had no idea he had that skill. It's a trait of the Kikuta family."

"The last thing I remember is his eyes. We gazed at each other and then I fell asleep."

After a pause Kaede went on: "He's gone, hasn't he?"

"My uncle, Muto Kenji, and the Kikuta master Kotaro came for him last night," Shizuka replied.

"And I will never see him again?" Kaede remembered her desperation the previous night, before the long, deep sleep. She had begged Takeo not to leave her. She had been terrified of her future without him, angry and wounded by his rejection of her. But all that turbulence had been stilled.

"You must forget him," Shizuka said, taking Kaede's hand in hers and stroking it gently. "From now on, his life and yours cannot touch."

Kaede smiled slightly. *I cannot forget him*, she was thinking.

Nor can he ever be taken from me. I have slept in ice. I have seen the White Goddess.

"Are you all right?" Shizuka said again, with urgency. "Not many people survive the Kikuta sleep. They are usually dispatched before they wake. I don't know what it has done to you."

"It hasn't harmed me. But it has altered me in some way. I feel as if I don't know anything—as if I have to learn everything anew."

Shizuka knelt before her, puzzled, her eyes searching Kaede's face. "What will you do now? Where will you go? Will you return to Inuyama with Arai?"

"I think I should go home to my parents. I must see my mother. I'm so afraid she died while we were delayed in Inuyama for all that time. I will leave in the morning. I suppose you should inform Lord Arai."

"I understand your anxiety," Shizuka replied, "but Arai may be reluctant to let you go."

"Then I shall have to persuade him," Kaede said calmly. "First I must eat something. Will you ask them to prepare some food? And bring me some tea, please."

"Lady." Shizuka bowed to her and stepped off the

veranda. As she walked away Kaede heard the plaintive notes of a flute played by some unseen person in the garden behind the temple. She thought she knew the player, one of the young monks from the time when they had first visited the temple to view the famous Sesshu paintings, but she could not recall his name. The music spoke to her of the inevitability of suffering and loss. The trees stirred as the wind rose, and owls began to hoot from the mountain.

Shizuka came back with the tea and poured a cup for Kaede. She drank as if she were tasting it for the first time, every drop having its own distinct, smoky flavor against her tongue. And when the old woman who looked after guests brought rice and vegetables cooked with bean curd, it was as if she had never tasted food before. She marveled silently at the new powers that had been awakened within her.

"Lord Arai wishes to speak with you before the end of the day," Shizuka said. "I told him you were not well, but he insisted. If you do not feel like facing him now, I will go and tell him again."

"I am not sure we can treat Lord Arai in that fashion," Kaede said. "If he commands me, I must go to him."

"He is very angry," Shizuka said in a low voice. "He is

offended and outraged by Takeo's disappearance. He sees in it the loss of two important alliances. He will almost certainly have to fight the Otori now, without Takeo on his side. He'd hoped for a quick marriage between you—"

"Don't speak of it," Kaede interrupted. She finished the last of the rice, placed the eating sticks down on the tray, and bowed in thanks for the food.

Shizuka sighed. "Arai has no real understanding of the Tribe—how they work, what demands they place on those who belong to them."

"Did he never know that you were from the Tribe?"

"He knew I had ways of finding things out, of passing on messages. He was happy enough to make use of my skills in forming the alliance with Lord Shigeru and Lady Maruyama. He had heard of the Tribe, but like most people he thought they were little more than a guild. That they should have been involved in Iida's death shocked him profoundly, even though he profited from it." She paused and then said quietly, "He has lost all trust in me: I think he wonders how he slept with me so many times without being assassinated himself. Well, we will certainly never sleep together again. That is all over."

"Are you afraid of him? Has he threatened you?"

"He is furious with me," Shizuka replied. "He feels I have betrayed him—worse: made a fool out of him. I do not think he will ever forgive me." A bitter note crept into her voice. "I have been his closest confidante, his lover, his friend, since I was hardly more than a child. I have borne him two sons. Yet, he would have me put to death in an instant were it not for your presence."

"I will kill any man who tries to harm you," Kaede said.

Shizuka smiled. "How fierce you look when you say that!"

"Men die easily." Kaede's voice was flat. "From the prick of a needle, the thrust of a knife. You taught me that."

"But you are yet to use those skills, I hope," Shizuka replied, "though you fought well at Inuyama. Takeo owes his life to you."

Kaede was silent for a moment. Then she said in a low voice, "I did more than fight with the sword. You do not know all of it."

Shizuka stared at her. "What are you telling me? That it was you who killed Iida?" she whispered.

Kaede nodded. "Takeo took his head, but he was already dead. I did what you told me. He was going to rape me."

Shizuka grasped her hands. "Never let anyone know that! Not one of these warriors, not even Arai, would let you live."

"I feel no guilt or remorse," Kaede said. "I never did a less shameful deed. Not only did I protect myself but the deaths of many were avenged: Lord Shigeru; my kinswoman, Lady Maruyama, and her daughter; and all the other innocent people whom Iida tortured and murdered."

"Nevertheless, if this became generally known, you would be punished for it. Men would think the world turned upside down if women start taking up arms and seeking revenge."

"My world is already turned upside down," Kaede said. "Still, I must go and see Lord Arai. Bring me . . ." She broke off and laughed. "I was going to say, 'bring me some clothes,' but I have none. I have nothing!"

"You have a horse," Shizuka replied. "Takeo left the gray for you."

"He left me Raku?" Kaede smiled, a true smile that illuminated her face. She stared into the distance, her eyes dark and thoughtful.

"Lady?" Shizuka touched her on the shoulder.

"Comb out my hair and send a message to Lord Arai to say I will visit him directly."

❖

It was almost completely dark by the time they left the women's rooms and went toward the main guest rooms where Arai and his men were staying. Lights gleamed from the temple, and farther up the slope, beneath the trees, men stood with flaring torches around Lord Shigeru's grave. Even at this hour people came to visit it, bringing incense and offerings, placing lamps and candles on the ground around the stone, seeking the help of the dead man who every day became more of a god to them.

He sleeps beneath a covering of flame, Kaede thought, herself praying silently to Shigeru's spirit for guidance, while she pondered what she should say to Arai. She was the heir to both Shirakawa and Maruyama; she knew Arai would be seeking some strong alliance with her, probably some marriage that would bind her into the power he was amassing. They had spoken a few times during her stay at Inuyama, and again on the journey, but Arai's attention had been taken up with securing the countryside and his strategies for the future. He had not shared these with her, beyond expressing his desire for the Otori marriage to take place. Once—a life-time ago, it seemed now—she had wanted to be more than a pawn in the hands of the warriors who commanded her fate. Now, with the newfound strength that the icy sleep had given her, she resolved again to take control of her life. *I need time,* she thought. *I must do nothing rashly. I must go home before I make any decisions.*

One of Arai's men—she remembered his name was Niwa—greeted her at the veranda's edge and led her to the doorway. The shutters all stood open. Arai sat at the end of the room, three of his men next to him. Niwa spoke her name and the warlord looked up at her. For a moment they studied each other. She held his gaze and felt power's strong pulse in her veins. Then she dropped to her knees and bowed to him, resenting the gesture yet knowing she had to appear to submit.

He returned her bow, and they both sat up at the same time. Kaede felt his eyes on her. She raised her head and gave him the same unflinching look. He could not meet it. Her heart was pounding at her audacity. In the past she had both liked and trusted the man in front of her. Now she saw changes in his face. The lines had deepened around his mouth and eyes. He had been both pragmatic and flexible, but now he was in the grip of his intense desire for power.

Not far from her parents' home, the Shirakawa flowed through vast limestone caves where the water had formed pillars and statues. As a child she was taken there every year to worship the goddess who lived within one of these pillars under the mountain. The statue had a fluid, living shape, as though the spirit that dwelt within were trying to break out from beneath the covering of lime. She thought of that stone covering now. Was power a limy river calcifying those who dared to swim in it?

Arai's physical size and strength made her quail inwardly, reminding her of that moment of helplessness in Iida's arms, of the strength of men who could force women in any way they wanted. *Never let them use that strength*, came the thought, and then: *Always be armed*. A taste came into her mouth, as sweet as persimmon, as strong as blood: the knowledge and taste of power. Was this what drove men to clash endlessly with each other, to enslave and destroy each other? Why should a woman not have that too?

13

She stared at the places on Arai's body where the needle and the knife had pierced Iida, had opened him up to the world he'd tried to dominate and let his life's blood leak away. *I must never forget it*, she told herself. *Men also can be killed by women. I killed the most powerful warlord in the Three Countries.*

All her upbringing had taught her to defer to men, to submit to their will and their greater intelligence. Her heart was beating so strongly, she thought she might faint. She breathed deeply, using the skills Shizuka had taught her, and felt the blood settle in her veins.

"Lord Arai, tomorrow I will leave for Shirakawa. I would be very grateful if you will provide men to escort me home."

"I would prefer you to stay in the East," he said, slowly. "But that is not what I want to talk to you about first." His eyes narrowed as he stared at her. "Otori's disappearance: Can you shed any light on this extraordinary occurrence? I believe I have established my right to power. I was already in alliance with Shigeru. How can young Otori ignore all obligations to me and to his dead father? How can he disobey and walk away? And where has he gone? My men have been searching the district all day, as far as Yamagata. He's completely vanished."

"I do not know where he is," she replied.

"I'm told he spoke to you last night before he left."

"Yes," she said simply.

"He must have explained to you at least—"

"He was bound by other obligations." Kaede felt sorrow build within her as she spoke. "He did not intend to insult you." Indeed, she could not remember Takeo mentioning Arai to her, but she did not say this.

"Obligations to the so-called Tribe?" Arai had been controlling his anger, but now it burst fresh into his voice, into his eyes. He moved his head slightly, and she guessed he was looking past her to where Shizuka knelt in the shadows on the veranda. "What do you know of them?"

"Very little," she replied. "It was with their help that Lord Takeo climbed into Inuyama. I suppose we are all in their debt in that respect."

Speaking Takeo's name made her shiver. She recalled the feel of his body against hers, at that moment when they both expected to die. Her eyes darkened, her face softened. Arai was aware of it, without knowing the reason, and when he spoke again she heard something else in his voice besides rage.

"Another marriage can be arranged for you. There are

15

other young men of the Otori, cousins to Shigeru. I will send envoys to Hagi."

"I am in mourning for Lord Shigeru," she replied. "I cannot consider marriage to anyone. I will go home and recover from my grief." *Will anyone ever want to marry me, knowing my reputation*, she wondered, and could not help following with the thought: *Takeo did not die.* She had thought Arai would argue further, but after a moment he concurred.

"Maybe it's best that you go to your parents. I will send for you when I return to Inuyama. We will discuss your marriage then."

"Will you make Inuyama your capital?"

"Yes. I intend to rebuild the castle." In the flickering light his face was set and brooding. Kaede said nothing. He spoke again abruptly. "But to return to the Tribe: I had not realized how strong their influence must be. To make Takeo walk away from such a marriage, such an inheritance, and then to conceal him completely . . . to tell you the truth, I had no idea what I was dealing with." He glanced again toward Shizuka.

He will kill her, she thought. *It's more than just anger at Takeo's disobedience: His self-esteem has been deeply wounded too. He must suspect*

Shizuka has been spying on him for years. She wondered what happened to the love and desire that had existed between them. Had it all dissolved overnight? Did the years of service, the trust, and loyalty, all come to nothing?

"I shall make it my business to find out about them," he went on, almost as if he were speaking to himself. "There must be people who know, who will talk. I cannot let such an organization exist. They will undermine my power as the white ant chews through wood."

Kaede said, "I believe it was you who sent Muto Shizuka to me, to protect me. I owe my life to that protection. And I believe I kept faith with you in Noguchi Castle. Strong bonds exist between us and they shall be unbroken. Whoever I marry will swear allegiance to you. Shizuka will remain in my service and will come with me to my parents' home."

He looked at her then, and again she met his gaze with ice in her eyes. "It's barely thirteen months since I killed a man for your sake," he said. "You were hardly more than a child. You have changed. . . ."

"I have been made to grow up," she replied. She made an effort not to think of her borrowed robe, her complete lack of possessions. *I am the heir to a great domain,* she told herself.

continued to hold his eyes until he reluctantly inclined his head.

"Very well. I will send men with you to Shirakawa, and you may take the Muto woman."

"Lord Arai." Only then did she drop her eyes and bow.

Arai called to Niwa to make arrangements for the following day, and Kaede bade him good night, speaking with great deference. She felt she had come out of the encounter well; she could afford to pretend that all power lay on his side.

She returned to the women's rooms with Shizuka, both of them silent. The old woman had already spread out the beds, and now she brought sleeping garments for them before helping Shizuka undress Kaede. Wishing them good night, she retired to the adjoining room.

Shizuka's face was pale and her demeanor more subdued than Kaede had ever known it. She touched Kaede's hand and whispered, "Thank you," but said nothing else. When they were both lying beneath the cotton quilts, as mosquitoes whined around their heads and moths fluttered against the lamps, Kaede could feel the other woman's body rigid next to hers, and knew Shizuka was struggling with grief. Yet, she did not cry.

Kaede reached out and put her arms around Shizuka, holding her closely without speaking. She shared the same deep sorrow but no tears came to her eyes. She would allow nothing to weaken the power that was coming to life within her.